American Diaries

NELL DUNNE

ELLIS ISLAND, 1904

⚬⚬⚬

by Kathleen Duey

⚬⚬⚬

Aladdin Paperbacks

New York   London   Toronto   Sydney   Singapore

For Richard
For Ever

First Aladdin Paperbacks edition August 2000

Copyright © 2000 by Kathleen Duey

Aladdin Paperbacks
An imprint of Simon & Schuster
Children's Publishing Division
1230 Avenue of the Americas
New York, NY 10020

The text for this book was set in Fairfield Light
Printed and bound in the United States of America

10 9 8 7 6 5 4 3 2 1

Library of Congress Catalog Card Number: 00-105323
ISBN 0-689-83555-8

February 12, 1904, still aboard the Astoria

Another fierce and gloomy day. Yesterday, Granny Rose talked nonsense again most of the day. She is much worse now than she ever was at home. She's talking to herself more, too. I can see it worries Mama, but she says nothing.

How I am coming to hate this ship. It's so cold this past week. At least right now the Englishman and his mean-eyed wife are still asleep and silent on their side of the curtain. It's nice not to have to listen to them argue.

Little Fiona, Mama, and Granny Rose are sleeping, all in Mama's cot, sharing the blankets. Granny Rose is curled up around Fiona.

So many are sick now, mostly stomach trouble since the seas got rough last week. But some are coughing and sneezing, and a few sound like they are close to getting pneumonia. Mama keeps saying we mustn't get sick. She is so worried that the Americans will turn us around and send us home to County Mayo. I wish we could go home. As I write that, though, my very bones take a chill. I want to get off this cold gray ocean more than I have ever wanted anything. To think about being sent back out on it makes me feel ill.

We should come into port tomorrow morning, people are saying. They have said it before, though, twice. Oh, how I hope it is true this time.

Last evening, before the meal was meted out (slops again, meat so stale it made Granny Rose decide not to eat—the food is worse every day), I tried going up on deck. The officer was stationed at the stair top as usual. He never says a word to anyone so long as we don't try to go up onto the broad deck the first-class passengers use. I like to watch them. They tuck up their furs and stand in the wind, staring off to sea like they can see something the rest of us can't. Or maybe they can. They can see a point in all this tossing and swaying, I suppose, because they know that even if they get sick now, they won't be cold or hungry once we land.

In his last letter Da said we would all have to work very hard, especially Patrick because he's the boy and oldest as well. He charged me with making sure Granny Rose made it to America all right, and Patrick with guarding us all from harm. I have been trying so hard to make Granny Rose eat well, but the food is all stale now.

I am frightened. So is Mama, I can tell. As I have written in this journal nearly every day for the three long weeks and more since we left home, I did not want to come to America! All I want is to go back to the little farm in Ballinrobe, in dear County Mayo. I want to run the road up to Caitlin's house and knock and have her mother ask me in for tea. I want to smell the wet grass and the sharp odor of the potatoes lying in the sun waiting for us to go back over them, rubbing the soil off before we bundle them for the storeroom. And I want Papa to be with us. It is a terrible sorrow being separated from him, but why couldn't he come home, instead of making us travel to New York City to live?

I know why, of course. It is because he wants to own a farm, not just rent one. And he says in America we shall—but never back in Ireland, not even with the land reforms.

Fiona just stirred in her sleep, but then she settled again. I am glad. I love this tiny bit of quiet early in the mornings. Patrick will be along soon, loping the corridors like a colt, restless and gangling. He has grand visions of becoming a wealthy and important man in America—like Andrew Carnegie, he says. That old Scotsman's name is known everywhere—the steel king of America. I have no such dream. I would be happy to go home, if I could bear the thought of another journey as cold and awful as this one has been. If Granny Rose is somehow refused entry—I am the one who will have to go back with her. I just know it.

I made a friend four days past. Mary is a Scot from Loch Leven, traveling with just her older brothers, Will and Angus. They are orphans, their parents dead of fever last winter, and not a soul in their family well-off enough to take them in besides an uncle living in America now. At first Mary said little about herself. Then, yesterday, she told me everything. She says she is going to be an actress in her uncle's troupe in New York! I cannot imagine saying lines on a stage while people sat and watched. She absolutely lights up when she talks about it, though. I have not told Mama, of course. Mama already doesn't like Mary much because her manners are not very strict.

Mary says her uncle has told them about America—how the rich and poor touch shoulders on the streets. She says that anyone can ride the new tunnel trains and go all over the city.

People tell all sorts of tales. It is impossible to know what is really true. I have heard the Englishman on the other side of our curtain telling his wife that people are beaten up, that no one is fed for days, and that some of those who die on Ellis Island are just thrown into the sea. Patrick said he heard something like that in the single men's section—but he said, too, that some of the younger men are just seeing whom they can scare.

Ellis Island. It sounds harmless enough. Mama pretends she knows all about it, but she is just reading and rereading Father's letter about his own crossing two and a half years ago. He says we will be let off on the

Manhattan docks first. Then we'll be ferried out to the island with its inspectors, then we will be taken back again.

I only hope that sour-faced old Englishman next door is wrong about what happens on Ellis Island. He hates the Irish and frowns every time he has to speak to us for one reason or another. His wife is worse. She looks past us as though we were thin air. I have no love for the English either, but I have manners, after all.

Two years. I can hardly believe it has been so long since I have seen Father. I will know Da, of course, but wonder if he will know me. I have grown a great deal and my hair has gotten longer and heavier. I am nearly as tall as Mama is; everyone says I look like her when she was a girl. So I suppose he will know me. Still, the idea that he might not makes me feel very odd inside my heart. Oh, how I just wish we would arrive and be off this smelly ship.

Fiona just this moment stirred again. Granny Rose nearly woke up. I wish I could turn the gas lamp up a little, but I am afraid it would wake them. I hope all three of them sleep on another hour or two. I wish I were still little like Fiona. She blinks her big blue eyes and just trusts that we will all take care of her.

CHAPTER ONE

Nell rolled her pen up in the soft cotton cloth that served as a holder, then corked her inkwell. It was so cold. She blew into her hands, trying to warm them as she glared at the paper. Her handwriting was never very neat and it was worse now with her freezing hands and the unending sway of the ship. Writing brought her comfort, but she knew she should do less of it; she should save her ink. Money was going to be hard to come by. This bottle would have to last a long time.

Nell put on her scarf. Pressed close against her scalp, her ears felt like crescents of ice. She tightened her coat as well as she could with the mismatched belt. The coat was an old one of Patrick's, drab gray and boyish, but it was thick pounded wool, soft and warm. She ran her hands down her front to smooth the coat as best she could. It was actually better than the one Patrick wore now; it had been bought before everyone in the family was scraping and saving to pay for passage to America.

A banging sound in the corridor pulled Nell from her thoughts. She stood slowly, her legs cramped from being bent beneath her in the chair. Her stockings did little to keep the cold air from her ankles as she faced the door, then glanced back at Mama, Fiona, and Granny Rose. They were all still breathing slowly and softly.

Nell felt a physical ache, a longing for fresh air, air that didn't smell of gaslights and hundreds of unwashed people. She turned the door handle carefully. The catch was silent if she moved it slowly enough—she'd had a lot of practice in the past two weeks. Someone was always asleep. None of them slept well enough at night to stay awake all day—not even Patrick over on the men's side. He was in the single men's dormitory. He was in a top berth with two Hungarian brothers in the two below him. He said they both snored like rumbling thunderstorms, and they argued constantly. He could no more understand their debates than they could understand his requests that they quiet down.

As she stepped out of the tiny compartment, Nell closed the door behind herself as slowly as she had opened it, making sure the latch caught. If Fiona woke, the important thing would be to keep her inside the room. She had just begun figuring out door handles over the last two months. She was tall for an eighteen-month-old baby and very smart.

A thin nasal wailing came from behind the closed door across the corridor. Nell knew now that it was the family saying prayers. They said them three or four times a day and she wanted to ask them what the prayers meant, but none of them spoke a word of English. The first three days she had thought that someone was hurt or dead, and that they were grieving, wailing their strange half songs. Patrick was the one who had set her straight. How he found out was anyone's guess.

Nell turned up the narrow corridor and closed her eyes for an instant. Her sickness from the swaying of the ship wasn't nearly as bad as Granny Rose's, but the narrow corridors were the worst places for her. It seemed like the walls themselves slanted and then righted themselves and her whole mind screamed that she was about to fall down. She had learned to walk with her hands out at her sides, ready to steady herself if the *Astoria* caught a swell and rocked hard to one side.

A man stepped out of one of the rooms and Nell had to stop abruptly to keep from running into him. He wore a turban, but he had on trousers, not those drapery-looking robes like the people they had seen waiting for another ship in Liverpool. Patrick had said they were from India. Someone else had said they were Arabic. Nell grimaced as the man cleared his throat, then spat on the floor. A lot of the men did it, from every country, and it always made her stomach tighten.

"Nell?"

It was Mary's voice and Nell turned instantly, grateful for company. Mary's fair skin was pink with the chill, her blond hair well hidden beneath a tattered fur hat. Her dress was old, too, but extravagant, a dark blue wool with worn white piping on the sleeves and collar.

"You look upset," Mary said in a quieter voice as she got closer. "Did you see a rat?"

Nell shook her head and tightened her scarf, feeling the chilled rims of her ears like ice against her head again. She rubbed her hands together as Mary came up the corridor.

"Last night I saw a huge one," Mary said. "It ran into one of those high vent holes." She shuddered, then smiled. "Have you been above decks?"

Nell shook her head, not wanting to think about the ship's rats. "I haven't been on deck since the day before yesterday."

Mary shivered dramatically, her eyes closing. "It's so cold."

"Have you been up there?" Nell asked, even though she already knew the answer.

Mary nodded. "Of course, but only for a minute. It's a nasty wind."

Nell nodded. "Maybe I won't go up at all today." But as she spoke the words she knew she had to, even if it was miserably, terribly cold. On the days of the last storm she had not gone up into the free air and she had begun to feel like the ship was a coffin, with herself trapped inside. "I think about all the water beneath us sometimes," she said aloud.

"You must stop thinking morbid thoughts," Mary scolded. She smiled, but her usually cheery face seemed strained and Nell knew she had thought about the ocean beneath them, too.

"Want to come back up with me?" Nell asked.

Mary nodded, so Nell started off again. It was hard not to think grim thoughts. It seemed to her like they had been aboard the *Astoria* forever. She was desperate to get off the ship, and yet terrified to have the voyage end. Both feelings washed over her like the endless gray waves.

"Wait for me," Mary called out.

"I'm sorry," Nell apologized, slowing.

Mary was reaching up to pull the old fur hat down around her temples as she hurried to catch up. "You're nearly running."

Nell smiled. Mary's Scots accent thickened into

near impenetrable density when she wasn't thinking about it.

"Now, let's start even and I will keep up," Mary teased. "I didn't know it was a race."

"I am just dying for a breath of fresh air," Nell told her. "I'm used to being on the farm. The insides of this ship are so close-quartered."

"And so smelly," Mary added.

"Indeed," Nell agreed, her stomach tightening as the corridor leaned to one side, then slowly righted itself. She said a silent prayer to the Virgin Mother that the seas would not rise as high as they had the week before. "Are you scared about Ellis Island?" she asked, suddenly needing to talk about it to someone besides her family. "My father said in his letter that it isn't so hard as some say."

"It had better not be," Mary said quietly. "My brothers will never forgive me if I don't make it through. One would have to go back with me. And neither wants to. You may bet on that with your last coin and win."

"I've thought of that with Granny Rose," Nell admitted. "Patrick and Mother and Fiona would likely go on without me. I'd be the one."

They started up the steep steps and Nell nodded politely at the officer who stood guard near the top, standing beside the locked gate that closed off the first-class section of the ship. "We thought we would get a little air," Nell murmured. "If we may?"

"Just stay back from the railing," he said curtly.

Nell was startled. None of the officers had ever spoken a word to her. She had heard them shout warnings at Patrick and his friends if they got noisy or dared to stare up at the quality girls. Mostly the officers just stood with rigid posture, looking irritated, and made sure the people from steerage who dared come up on this narrow, windy strip of deck didn't annoy the first-class passengers pacing the sheltered promenades above them.

"We had an old man very nearly fall over the side about an hour past," the officer added without turning to look at them. He lifted his chin and stared at the horizon. "Decks are all iced over. It's turned colder."

"Thank you for the warning, sir," Mary said in her stilted imitation of an English top-drawer wealthy girl.

"How many different accents can you mimic?" Nell asked as they edged out of the stairwell. The freezing air bit at her lips and nose and when she tried to smile at Mary, her teeth ached in the cold.

"I've never counted. Ten or twelve, I suppose. My uncle taught me another every time he came to visit," Mary said, tucking her hands inside her pockets.

"I wish I had an uncle who was a stage actor," Nell said. "Everyone in my family is a farmer of one sort or another, though, and they'd probably disapprove of anyone who wasn't." Nell hunched her shoulders up against the wind, grateful to be outside even though the weather was mean.

"My uncle has traveled all over the world, working in theaters," Mary said. "Angus and Will want to do that. I am going to talk them into taking me, too."

Nell blinked, turning a little out of the wind as she pulled in a deep breath of the icy air. She wanted to say that she would do the same, but she wasn't sure she ever wanted to cross another ocean; not unless her whole family decided to move back to Ireland one day. She smiled without showing her teeth this time. "Well, you are good at accents and you say you are good at acting, so they will probably want to take you."

"Oh, I do hope so," Mary answered, "It'd be the finest thing I can imagine."

Nell was astonished to hear Mary sound as Irish as anyone she had ever known at home in County Mayo. Nell watched Mary pull her hat down over her ears again. The fur had moth holes in it big enough to put her thumb through.

Mary was smiling. "But my uncle Alexander is the only interesting one in my whole family, Nell. Everyone else knows how to spin and weave wool. Nothing more."

"I can spin," Nell said. "I hate it."

Mary nodded. "That's what I mean, it's dull as dirt, and it is all my family knows—except for Alexander John Zeller Macrae—who is the best uncle in all the world. If it wasn't for him, we'd have been stuck spinning and weaving forever to earn our keep at Aunty Bess's."

Nell leaned against Mary and she leaned back. Between them there was a little warmth, at least one side of their bodies where the biting wind could not seep through to skin.

"We can't stay up here much longer," Nell said.

"I know," Mary answered, her eyes moving as she spoke. Nell followed her gaze and knew what she was doing.

"They said we'd see land soon."

Mary nodded instantly. "I heard that, too."

The wind whistled though the railings above their heads. Nell wondered for a moment if any of the wealthy people were out, peering into the cold gusts of salty wind to try to see the famous city of New York. Probably not. They would be inside, warm and cozy in just a sweater or two.

"We could get sick in this wind," Mary said, and Nell felt a sinking inside herself. Mary was right. It was foolish, coming up here to stand in a freezing gale like this. The idea of going back into the thick soup of smells and sounds below decks revolted her, but her teeth were already chattering and her knees felt almost frozen stiff.

"Come on," Mary said, and this time Nell nodded, turning to lead the way again. As they passed the ship's officer, he looked above their heads as usual, but when Nell heard him draw in a quick breath; she glanced back from the top step.

"There it is!" the officer was saying. "I will be glad to be shut of these stormy seas for a few days."

"There's what?" Nell asked.

The officer pointed without looking at them. "New York! I saw lights."

Nell turned as Mary did, both of them hurrying back out to the ice-clad railing. Nell blinked, straining to see, but the swells only rose and fell, lifting the ship upward, then letting it fall again while she stared at the horizon. She couldn't see anything but gray water and gray sky and it was impossible to tell where they met in the distance.

Nell heard Mary sigh in disappointment. Nell turned to glance back at the officer. Perhaps he had been tricking them. But his face didn't look unkind or taunting. In fact, it was as though he didn't see them at all. His eyes were fixed to the west.

Nell felt Mary's hand suddenly tighten on her arm. "Look!"

Nell turned. The grayness of the horizon was as empty as it had been before and she frowned and drew breath to speak, then caught herself. There, just for an instant, she had seen tiny flashes, sparkles come and gone so quickly that if she had blinked she would have missed them.

"See that?" the officer said. "That's one of the tall buildings. Probably some accountants are working early. Or very late," he added.

Nell saw the tiny pinpricks of light once more and heard Mary make a sound of delight. They exchanged a smile; then, as Nell turned back to watch for the sparkles of light again, it began to snow. Wind-driven pellets swirled and pelted her face, each one searing her skin with its cold.

The snow hushed the sound of the sea and the laboring engines in the depths of the ship. It was odd, as though someone had suddenly stuffed cotton in her ears. Nell swiped at her face, trying to see through the snowfall. She couldn't.

"I saw New York," Mary breathed. "We both did!"

Nell nodded. "Just for a second or so, but I did see the lights."

"This is it, then," Mary said in an unsteady voice. "We are almost there."

Nell tried to answer, but her voice caught and she could only stand still, overcome by a rush of tangled feelings. She knew she should run and tell Mama and Granny Rose, that she should be happy. But she wasn't.

"We should go tell someone," Mary said, echoing her thoughts. "We are the only two who know."

Nell nodded but didn't move. "Probably."

Mary made a soft sound. "I'm scared," she admitted.

Nell nodded again. "I am, too."

CHAPTER TWO

Halfway down the stairs, Nell heard the breakfast bell just as the dense wall of human odors hit her nose. Mary usually wrinkled her face and made a joke about the stink, but today, she flashed Nell a smile and began to run. Nell kept up, skidding to a stop in front of her door. Mary called a farewell and ran on, headed for the single women's dormitory.

Nell made a point of not looking beyond the curtain as she came in. It infuriated the English woman that they had to use the same door. Nell knew they were lucky. The dormitories had a few hundred bunks in one long room.

There was a stirring on the cot as Mama rolled over, yawning hugely. Granny Rose made an irritated sound and shifted on the narrow cot. That woke Fiona and she began to whimper.

"Breakfast bell," Nell said quickly, so her mother and grandmother wouldn't think she had awakened them by accident. "It just rang." Fiona's whimper strengthened into a louder cry.

"Run along first and save our table in the back if you can get it," Mama said as she stood.

Granny Rose was sitting up, one hand pressed against the small of her back. "We'll hurry, Nell."

Nell nodded, glad to be sent out of the too small room while Mama changed Fiona's diaper and wrung the urine out into the little washbasin, then hung the diaper to dry. There was no way to wash the soiled cotton rags easily, though the ship did provide washtubs in a little room with a floor drain. The trouble was, the soap was strong enough to eat a baby's skin off and it was impossible to rinse the cloth out well enough in the gray, reused water.

Nell paused at the door. "This is our last morning," she said aloud.

Granny Rose looked up and Mama paused.

Nell took a deep breath. "We saw lights. I was up there with Mary and we saw—"

"I would like you to stay clear of that girl, Nell," Mama said sternly. "She is rude and brash."

"You saw lights where?" Granny Rose interrupted.

Nell smiled at the eager expression on Granny Rose's face. Sometimes she looked almost like a girl.

"On the horizon, just before the snow started again. It's so cold up there it hurts to breathe, almost."

Mama looked up from changing Fiona. "Are we there, then?"

"The officer said we had a few hours."

Mama frowned. "I don't want you running around this ship like that. I thought you were going to write in your book and—"

"I did," Nell interrupted, and Mama scowled at her.

"See? You get around that girl and you start being rude to your mother."

"I am sorry, Mama," Nell said dutifully.

"Thank you, daughter," Mama said. "Now run for a table before they are all gone."

"What lights?" Granny Rose demanded. Nell looked at her. She was usually confused for a few minutes after she awakened.

"I'll explain it all to her," Mama said, making a shooing motion with one hand.

Nell nodded and went out the door, catching a glimpse of Granny Rose's bewildered face. She was ready to get off this ship, too. They all were.

"Excuse me," someone said from behind her and Nell flattened herself against the door to let a tall man with white hair pass. She had noticed him in the dining room several times. His abnormally white skin and pale eyes made him stand out; he looked like a man covered in frost. As he walked away Nell stared at him. She hadn't known that he spoke English and it surprised her. In fact, she thought, following him down the corridor toward the dining room, it surprised her that he spoke at all. She wasn't sure she had ever seen him talking to anyone.

The crowd thickened with every step. Nell turned a corner and hurried along, passing the door of the women's dormitory. She glanced in, but Mary wasn't near her bunk—on the third tier toward the middle. The huge room was full of women sitting on their beds, or lying flat, staring at the ceiling.

Nell turned away and walked a little faster. Breakfast was served twice every morning and people could go to either session. The second was often more crowded, but this morning even fewer than usual had gotten up early because of the cold. Maybe she still had a chance to get their favorite table.

Almost running, Nell skimmed along the corridor, dodging around an old woman who stood alone, leaning against the wall, then a young woman who walked with three little children trailing out behind her like ducklings. The smallest child was talking in quick precise words, as though arguing with herself. Nell couldn't understand a word and wondered what language the little girl was speaking. She was four or five and lovely, with full cheeks, dark skin, and a long braid of dark hair that fell to her tiny waist. She wore an odd little dress that looked like it had been wrapped around her instead of seamed and sewn.

Nell smiled as she passed them. The first five or six days on the ship, she had noticed everyone. The white-haired man had caught her eye the first meal. And the men in long black coats with curving twists of hair that lay along their cheeks, showing from beneath round little hats. She had stared at women like the one she had just passed, marveling at the strangeness of their clothes. Then she had noticed the passengers less and less with every passing day as the food got worse and the seas rose—and the stink in the corridors got thicker.

"Only one more half-cold breakfast," she whispered to herself as she turned into the dining room.

"There you are," Mary's high-pitched voice came from the far side of the big room. She had seated herself at the table Mama liked best and now she was standing up and waving. Nell pressed her lips together. Mama was not going to like this.

Nell sat down. On the far side of the room, the silent waiters were starting to bring in food. It was in tins.

"It will be nice to eat food that doesn't taste like metal," she said aloud.

Mary's eyes were dancing. "Oh, there are a thousand things that will be wonderful!"

Nell smiled at Mary's exuberance and then glanced toward the door.

Mary followed her gaze. "Is your family coming?"

Nell nodded. "Mama and Granny Rose and Fiona. I don't know what Patrick is doing yet. He hasn't come to tell us."

Mary nodded. "I haven't seen my brothers either. I walked down that way, but the officer was on post so I had to come back."

"You wouldn't go into the men's dormitory, anyway," Nell scolded.

Mary shook her head. "Of course not. But I would have waited outside or asked someone to get them. I just wish they would come find me. Maybe once the rumor spreads that far," she trailed off, grinning. "How long do you think it might take? Half an hour? There are nearly two thousand passengers in steerage and—"

"How do you know that?" Nell interrupted.

Mary just laughed.

"I asked an officer. It's no secret, Nell."

Nell shook her head. Mary would walk up to anyone anywhere and ask for exactly what she wanted. Nell wished she could be less shy.

The bright coo and laugh of a baby made Nell turn; it was Fiona in Mama's arms, smiling a four-toothed smile. Mama and Granny Rose were coming toward them. Mama nodded curtly at Mary, who made a grand bowing gesture. "I saved it for you."

Mama looked startled. "What?"

"The table. I saved it for you," Mary repeated.

She turned her head slightly and winked at Nell.

"You saved it?"

Nell nodded. "She was here before me, Mama."

Mama sat down heavily, Fiona wriggling in her arms. Nell got up to help Granny Rose with the heavy chair.

"Coffee?" the waiter said, coming close. His apron was stained and his hands looked dirty. Nell had heard that the steerage waiters were men who hadn't had the fare to buy a ticket. None of them was much good at carrying the tins.

"Tea would be better," Granny Rose said in a low voice. The man heard her.

"Sorry, old lady, we don't have tea. The English are furious about it, too."

"I am not English!" Granny Rose told him.

The waiter laughed gently. "All right, then. All right. Do you want coffee?"

"No!" Granny Rose said emphatically.

"I would please," Mary said brightly.

"And myself," Mama said. "And potatoes for all of us."

Mary's eyes narrowed. "I can order for myself, please," she said, her eyes on Mama.

Nell watched her mother nod wearily. "Do so, then."

Mary looked at the waiter. "Potatoes, please."

Mama sighed and shot Nell a disapproving look.

Nell knew that this was exactly the kind of thing she didn't like about Mary. Nell bit her lip. Mary's insistence on doing things her own way made her feel uneasy, too, but not in the same way as Mama. Nell wished she could be more like Mary.

The waiter set down four tins and walked on, hauling the heavy straight-sided bucket with him. He would give out the tins until they were gone, then go get more. The last few tins were always cold, but it did no good to complain. Granny Rose had tried.

"Nell tells us only a few hours left," Mama said in a polite voice, shifting Fiona from her lap to a chair beside her, turned backward so that she could support herself standing up. Mama kept her left hand on Fiona's back, her right hand free to open her tin. She handed Fiona a potato. Nell watched Fiona set to work eating it. Her stomach wasn't upset today.

Nell uncovered her food and saw a little steam. She was grateful.

"Lovely to put her down for a bit," Mama said.

Nell nodded. Fiona was getting too big to be held all the time like this, but Mama refused to let her toddle around the ship. The floors were too dirty.

Nell sighed. It wouldn't be long before Mama asked her to hold her sister, she was sure. She dreaded it. When Fiona got restless it was really hard to keep her from wriggling loose and walking.

"One more day," Mary said, leaning forward to

address Fiona. Fiona turned her head away, then back, and put her thumb in her mouth with what was left of the potato. Mary grinned at her and Fiona smiled back.

"One more day," Granny Rose echoed. "That's what Patrick says, anyway."

"I thought you hadn't seen your brother today," Mary said, tilting her head.

"We haven't," Mama said tightly. Mary glanced at Nell, but Nell couldn't explain, not with Granny Rose sitting right there.

"Finish your potatoes before they get cold," Mama said to Nell, shooting a stern glance at Mary for good measure.

"Patrick said one more day, but he is often wrong, God love him," Granny Rose said. She set down her fork and Nell bent over her own tin, trying to eat fast. Once they were finished, Mama might let her walk back to the dormitory with Mary for a few minutes.

"He is the most stubborn husband a woman ever had," Granny Rose said, her eyes shining. "My Patrick," she added, speaking clearly so that she would be heard.

Mary glanced at Nell again. She shook her head slightly, a tiny motion that she hoped her mother would not see. Granny Rose fell back to eating and Nell let out her breath.

"We'll be in Dublin this morning?" Granny

Rose asked, lifting her head again.

Mary paused, her fork halfway to her mouth, then went on eating. Nell pretended not to notice. Mama was not going to want this discussed with a stranger she didn't like.

Nell chewed, her thoughts turning, her stomach tight. What if Granny Rose acted like this in front of the inspectors? Maybe they wouldn't care so much because she was an old woman. It wasn't like she would hurt anyone or cause any trouble. She just forgot things.

"Would you mind if Nell came back with me to the dormitory?" Mary asked very politely.

Nell waited for her mother to lift her head. "For a few minutes?"

Mary nodded, setting her fork across the tin and replacing the lid. "Yes, Mrs. Dunne. Just for a few minutes."

"If it's no more than that." Mama sighed heavily. "But come straight back to get your things together."

Mary was already on her feet. Nell stood up, too. Granny Rose didn't seem to notice that they were leaving. Nell let Mary lead the way and followed her closely. The dining room was filling up now and the noise of families and friends calling back and forth between the tables was rising.

"Can you feel it?" Mary said as they turned into the corridor. "The people, I mean?"

"Everyone is scared," Nell said. "Is that what you're talking about?"

Mary nodded, then frowned. "I am, but only a little."

Nell looked at her. It was probably true. Mary didn't seem to be too afraid of anything.

"Is your grandmother going crazy?" Mary asked abruptly.

Nell jerked around to face Mary. "No!" Then she pressed a finger to her lips. "Don't say that."

Mary shrugged. "There are no inspectors here, Nell. I just asked."

Nell shook her head. "She just forgets things sometimes."

"Like that your grandfather died?" Mary asked and Nell could hear the astonishment in her voice. "That's who she meant, isn't it?"

Nell nodded.

"And she forgets where she is going?"

"Yes," Nell said miserably. "And she talks to herself sometimes. She's been much worse since we left home."

Mary looked thoughtful. "I hadn't noticed it before this."

Nell nodded. "I have kept you from talking to Mama and Granny Rose for more than a minute," she admitted. "But Granny Rose is worst right after she wakes up."

Mary nodded. "Lots of old people are like that. My aunt forgets my name all the time," she said finally.

Nell tried to smile. "She isn't always forgetful either. Sometimes she's like she always was before Granddad died."

Mary nodded. "Don't worry, then. It will be fine."

Nell wished she could make herself believe it. But there was a knot in her stomach and it was tightening.

CHAPTER THREE

The dorm was noisy as usual. Nell sat on Mary's bunk, watching as she folded her clothes into her bag. Everyone seemed wild and fey this morning. Nell knew she was feeling everything more intensely than she cared to this morning; it was probably the same for all of them.

"I had better go. I promised Mama a few minutes," Nell said sadly.

Mary looked up at her. "We won't say good-bye, though. I will see you again."

Nell slid down from the second berth and they hugged. Nell found herself close to tears and she swallowed hard, embarrassed.

"We'll find each other somehow," Mary said finally, her own eyes sparkly with tears. "Do you know your new street number?"

Nell shook her head. "Mama doesn't even know the address. Da said he was moving in the last letter—

a bigger place for all of us. He will meet us at the first landing place. That's what his letter said."

Mary smiled. "I have no idea where my uncle lives. We are going to meet him at a restaurant named Wallace's back in New York. We won't see him until after we go through the Ellis Island inspectors."

"Why isn't he coming to meet you?" Nell asked.

Mary made a quick motion with one hand. "It doesn't matter. My brothers said we can find any address by asking people we pass."

Nell stared at her, at a loss for anything else to say. "I hope everything you dream about comes true for you," she said quietly.

Mary threw her arms around Nell and hugged her tightly again. Before Nell could respond, Mary had stepped back. "You'll come see me in a play someday. I will be famous."

Nell smiled, her eyes stinging. She would miss Mary a lot. It wasn't fair that she should make a friend and then lose her so quickly.

"You'd better go now," Mary said. "You don't want your mother upset at you today."

Nell nodded and hesitated, then whirled and crossed the crowded room. At the door she looked back. Mary was watching and they waved. Nell said a prayer going down the hall. She wanted to find Mary again in New York. She wanted at least one friend in this strange place.

When Nell got back to their compartment, Mama and Granny Rose were already there. She went in and closed the door. Then she set about emptying her bag and refolding her clothes. As she worked, she heard a clamor of voices in the corridor. She could imagine the passengers lining up. Some would have their bags already packed, ready to leave the ship the moment they could. But many would be trying to get a turn on the narrow deck above—a chance to see the city rising out of the gray waves, the land they had come so far to see. Nell longed to go up again, too. All she had seen was tiny flashes of light. But she knew Mama would never allow it.

When they heard the English couple stirring beyond the curtain that divided the cabin, Mama raised her voice and politely told them that breakfast was nearly over, and that it would not be long before the ship docked. There was a flurry of whispering in response and within five minutes, the couple left, dragging their trunk into the corridor, elbowing their way into the crowd.

Through the open door, Nell could see that people had left a narrow path on the other side of the corridor to allow those who had been up on deck to come back down again, single file. There was no other room to spare.

"Imagine that you saw America first!" Granny Rose said from behind her and Nell turned to smile, glad to be distracted from her uneasiness. Granny Rose seemed to be herself again.

"The lights were small," Nell said, "like some-one's porch lanterns a mile off. It was hard to be sure I had even seen anything at all." But she smiled as she said it. It *was* amazing that she had been the one to spot the light. Da would love the story; he would be proud of her.

Granny Rose beamed. "When your grandfather and I lived in that little house at the west end of Ballinrobe, I saw a shooting star one night."

Nell looked at her, wishing she could always sound just like this, clear and perfectly sensible.

"I was sleepless," Granny Rose went on. "Just walking the porch, worried over something, I think. And there was a flash like nothing I had ever seen."

"I remember you telling me about that once," Mama said. She was perched on the side of the bed, nursing Fiona. Nell smiled at her, too. She wished she could go back up and look again. Patrick would, of that she was sure. And when he came back he'd be as excited as a colt after a warm rain, and claiming he had seen something that no one else had seen.

"Those were good years," Granny Rose was saying. Nell turned around at the soft, dreamy tone of her voice as she smiled broadly and finished, her eyes sparkling. "I just know Patrick will be there to meet me."

Nell felt her stomach tighten. Granny Rose had

always been one of the smartest, sharpest-tongued women in all of County Mayo—maybe in all of Ireland. No one had ever dared cross her, but no one had ever been cheated by her, either. There were many men with less spine and spark than her grandmother. But now . . .

"Sean will come to meet us," Mama said quickly, and Nell nodded.

"My da will be there. Your son."

Granny looked offended. "I know that, Nell. And so will Patrick."

Her voice trailed off and Mama shot Nell a glance that warned her to be silent. There was little point in arguing with Granny Rose when she was mixing up now with then. Maybe, once they got settled in a new place and Granny Rose felt more at home again, it would happen less. Nell watched her grandmother turn aside and stand plucking at the front of her old woolen dress. She was murmuring something and Nell strained to hear her words, but couldn't.

A thunderous pounding on the door made them all jump. Granny Rose was startled out of her murmuring and Fiona started to cry. Nell whirled to face the door, her heart thudding, even though she knew who it must be.

Mama opened the door a crack, then all the way. Patrick spilled in from the crowded corridor, his face still flushed with cold. "You can see it now, the skyline with all the buildings jutting up," he said, grinning. "You can't imagine how tall some of them are. It's spectacular." He was breathing hard, and as he finished speaking he looked at them one by one and blinked, then cleared his throat. "Whatever is the matter with all of you? We're nearly there!"

Granny Rose walked forward and reached up to lay her hand on his cheek, patting him. Mama soothed Fiona, trying to get her to go back to sleep. She glanced up every few seconds to remind Patrick to keep his voice down. Patrick endured Granny Rose's patting as long as he could and then stepped back. "You'll freeze your hand, Granny Rose, my cheeks are cold as the wind this morning."

Granny Rose peered into his face. "Patrick, you have gotten too tall."

Patrick met Nell's eyes over Granny Rose's head, questioning. She shrugged. She had no idea what to do when Granny Rose got like this. None of them did. Mama cleared her throat over the sound of Fiona's soft crying. "Well, he has been tall like that for a few years now, Mother Dunne. He is nearly sixteen."

Granny Rose frowned again, plainly irritated. She turned from Patrick and stood with her back to all of them again. Nell suddenly hated the tiny room, hated being cooped up, so much that she was almost eager to face the American inspectors. Anything would be better than staying another day on this smelly ship. There was a rustling sound in the wall and she knew it was one of the big rats that sometimes appeared in the corridors or scuttled along the floor in the dining hall.

"I would just like a decent cup of tea," Granny Rose said suddenly, raising her voice. "Does that seem too much for an old woman to ask?"

"Of course not, Mother Dunne," Mama said instantly, moving away from the cot where Fiona lay sleeping soundly again. Granny Rose smiled.

"I have always liked it when you call me that."

Mama smiled back and Nell could see the relief on her face. Granny Rose rarely stayed confused and grumpy for long—if no one argued with her.

"Tea is a perfectly reasonable request," Mama said in the same comforting tone she had been using to hush Fiona.

Patrick let out a long breath. "I will go and pack up my bags then."

Mama nodded. "Then come back and join us here. I want you close. I want us all together as we get off the ship. So don't dally with those rough boys you have made friends out of, do you understand?"

"I will be careful to stay close," Patrick promised, and Nell saw that he meant it. They both wanted to be able to tell Da that they had done the jobs he'd given them. Patrick's eyes were shining with excitement and purpose.

"Get thee gone," Mama said, laughing a little at Patrick's eager, wide-legged stance. "It will take some time to get back and forth with that crowd packed along the corridor."

Patrick nodded. "I'll get back to you as soon as I can. Don't worry, though. The officer said we had two hours before we got to the docks, maybe more."

"Clean up then," Mama was saying. "Give your face a wash and comb your hair. We should all look as nice as we can."

Nell could hear the anxiousness in her mother's voice. Granny Rose made an impatient sound deep in her throat, but she didn't say anything, Fiona began to whimper quietly.

"I'll be back then," Patrick repeated, but still it took him a few seconds to actually open the door. The people in the corridor were a solid wall. Patrick wedged his way between two women and turned back to wave as Mama closed the door.

"Get your bag straightened out, Nell," Mama said, and there was a tremor in her voice.

Nell kneeled beside her bag. She had little to pack, but she pulled out her best dress and thought about putting it on.

"No," Mama said, reading her thoughts from across the little room. "It's too thin, that one. You'd freeze."

Nell nodded, but she looked down at her drab

brown wool dress. There were patched holes along the hem. The cloth had come from an old coat of Mrs. McKenny's from church. The thought of their dear little church with the moss-softened stones of the walkway made her blink back tears. She did not want to be here. She wanted to be *home*.

CHAPTER FOUR

The sound of foghorns was muted, but constant. The corridor was packed, and the jumble of languages weighed against Nell's ears, even though people were talking in low voices. Her bag wasn't heavy, but she was tired of holding it. Patrick was carrying Mama's and his own. Granny Rose's clothes were in with Mama's. Nell took a deep breath. The air was so stale that she felt almost faint.

"Can anyone see anything yet?" Granny Rose hissed. She had her hand, fingers spread wide, pushed against the broad back of the man who stood ahead of her in the cramped, ragged line that jammed the corridor. He had stepped back twice onto her toes and she was determined that it wasn't going to happen again. Patrick stood sideways, using the breadth of his shoulders to give Mama enough room to hold Fiona safely against her.

"Can anyone up there see anything?" Granny Rose nearly shouted.

Nell sighed. It was the twentieth time that Granny Rose had asked the same thing. "I don't think so." Nell leaned close to answer, and the sour smell of Granny Rose's breath made her feel a little sick.

There was a sudden soft jarring of the ship and the crowd went silent for a moment, startled, then the babble of voices rose again, louder than it had been before. Seconds passed slowly and Nell began to count them to distract herself. She could hear the sound of someone retching and prayed whoever it was would not actually vomit. Her own stomach was uncertain enough.

Nell kept counting, her eyes fixed on the dark coat of the man in front of her. His white gold hair hung down over his collar. He was alone in the line and now she was sure that he had no family or friends on the ship. She had wondered a dozen times where he was from and what language he spoke. Now she knew: It was English. He didn't look English, or Irish or Scot. He looked more like the golden-haired people from the northern countries who spoke the sharp-edged words that sounded harsh even when they were smiling.

Nell shifted the strap of her bag on her shoulder and wondered what English sounded like to them. Was it too dull-edged? Just a batch of meaningless sounds with a strange rhythm? Nell tried to imagine what English would sound like to someone who did not speak it, but it was impossible.

There was another soft shift of the deck under Nell's feet and she shivered, even though she wasn't cold now. The press of people around her had heated the corridor. A third jolt rocked the floor, and she heard one woman cry out and then shout something she couldn't understand. Then, a cheer went up from the crowd, a wild, joyous shout that subsided into babble again after a few seconds.

"We're docked," Patrick said, grinning. "That must have been the ship bumping the pier."

Nell looked up at him, praying it was true. All her fears of Ellis Island had sunk beneath her desperate need to get off the ship. The air was too thick to breathe, and she forced herself to start counting again. She was on 593 when the sound of a ship's horn came again, so close that the people hushed into startled silence.

Nell breathed slowly, willing her pounding heart to slow. There was no place to go, nothing to do but wait. At least, squeezed in between people like this, she was warm for the first time in days. The man in front of her stepped back, bumping into her. He turned around as far as he could, apologizing, his too light eyes sincere and kind.

"How long before they let us off?" Granny Rose asked in a shrill voice that cut through the odd silence that had fallen. Her voice seemed to free everyone else's and the sound of a thousand conversations rose to fill the corridor again. But people spoke more softly and for that, Nell was grateful.

"They're getting the first- and second-class passengers off now," Patrick said.

Nell turned to stare at him. He nodded, then brushed his hair back off his forehead and switched Mama's bag from one shoulder to the other. His own was smaller, tucked beneath his arm. "Jimmy was talking to a ship's mate, one of the cooks. He said we might sit here for several hours. It all depends on the rich folks. If the inspectors go slow up above, then we'll just have to wait on them."

Hours? Nell thought, unable to imagine standing in the crowd for that much longer. She heard Mama make an impatient little sound and heard Fiona whimper a little and babble something in her soft voice. Mama answered her quietly, then looked up, her chin resting on Fiona's dark curls. "Could you hold her for a while, Patrick? Then Nell can take a turn."

Patrick handed Mama's bag to Nell and put his head into the loop of the strap of his own. Then he reached out and Fiona stared at him. He rarely held her, and as much as she liked him, Nell knew that she was scared by all the commotion—she was not going to want to leave Mama's arms.

"Go on to your brother," Mama said quietly,

repeating it three or four times, each time lifting Fiona with a little nudging movement of her arms. Patrick pasted a big grin on his face and cajoled Fiona as she looked at him, then at the strangers who surrounded her. Finally, Fiona put out her arms and Patrick lifted her free.

Instead of holding her close to his chest as Mama had been doing, he hoisted her upward, settling her on his shoulders, his hands firmly around her legs.

"You be careful," Mama cautioned.

Patrick nodded and jounced a little, a slight bend and straighten of his knees that made Fiona giggle. He did it again.

"You're a good boy, Patrick," Granny Rose said.

Nell glanced at her. Granny Rose was beaming up at Patrick, her eyes shining. Nell couldn't help but smile. It was wonderful when Granny Rose wasn't confused about who was who.

Nell closed her eyes for a few seconds and sighed. She had been so cold for so long, and now she was hot. Her woolen dress was damp with perspiration and it itched. She worked Mama's bag across her front and slipped the strap over her free shoulder. There. The weights balanced well enough.

Another shudder ran through the ship and everyone was caught off guard. Nell leaned hard against the white-haired man in front of her, then straightened and apologized, reaching to steady Granny Rose. No one had fallen; there was nowhere to fall.

A woman somewhere ahead of them in line began to sing, a strange, intricate melody with words Nell didn't understand. It was a sad melody, though, and Nell felt her eyes brim with tears at the plaintive sound of the woman's voice. Conversations stopped as everyone listened to the mournful tune. Behind them, she could hear someone sniffling, then crying softly. Seconds later a second voice, a quiet, wailing sound rose from the rear of the line, somewhere way back by the dormitories. The song seemed to go on forever. The woman singing had a beautiful voice, high, sweet, and clear. It carried perfectly down the long tunnel of the corridor. People shifted from one foot to the other, but almost no one spoke as she sang. When she was finally finished there was a moment of silence, then a man shouted from far back in the line.

"That was a spirit lifter, darlin'. And do you know another dirge?"

Everyone who spoke enough English to understand laughed aloud. Nell could not help but join in. The white-haired man turned and his strange ice-colored eyes met hers. He smiled. Nell smiled back at him and felt Mama's pinching grip on her shoulder.

"Nell!" she hissed it as the man turned back around.

Nell shrugged. "I didn't do anything wrong, Mama."

"You are smiling and flirting with a stranger, Nell Dunne."

Nell shook her head, embarrassed, but if the man heard Mama he pretended he hadn't and smiled once more before turning back around. There were people on all sides of them still laughing aloud.

"Mama, I was not flirting!" Nell whispered, leaning toward her mother.

Mama scowled. "A girl your age should not be talking to strange men at all," she countered, her eyes narrowed. She nodded knowingly. "For all you know he has lice!"

Nell nodded wearily. The last thing she wanted to do was argue. She faced forward and stared at the odd white blond hair hanging over the collar of the man's dark suit. A tug at her own hair startled her, but when she looked up, it was Fiona, reaching down from her perch on Patrick's shoulders. She was happy at least; the novelty of being up so high hadn't yet worn thin.

Nell lowered her eyes and stared at the black coat of the man in front of her again. She hoped he hadn't heard Mama's remark about lice. There were people who did have them, she had seen the scratching at their scalps—but it was hardly their fault in a place like this. No one could take a proper bath. She started to count again, this time moving her lips to help herself concentrate.

CHAPTER FIVE

When the man in front of her moved, Nell very nearly fell down. She had closed her eyes and was trying not to lean on Granny Rose. None of them had said a word in an hour or more. There was only the constant murmur of people talking—and it had gotten quieter and quieter, until she had actually been able to hear herself whispering numbers as she counted. Granny Rose had complained for a while, talking to herself. Then even her voice had faded and the sound of the ship's horns were audible again.

"Can you see anything?" Mama asked Patrick. He was still holding Fiona and Nell was grateful to him for taking such a long turn. She shrugged the bags up higher on her aching shoulders and winced. She longed to set them down, but there really wasn't anywhere to set them—the white-haired man was inches from her face and she could feel the breath of the woman behind her on her neck.

Patrick grimaced, then shrugged, lifting Fiona in a little nudge that made her laugh again. That was one blessing, Nell thought—or two, really. Fiona had not soiled herself or gotten hungry yet. Three, she told herself. Granny Rose was calm and quiet, and when Mama spoke to her she answered and made sense.

The line moved again and Nell heard women start shouting somewhere behind them. The argument was in a language she didn't understand. As the voices quieted, she wondered about Mary and felt ashamed that she hadn't thought of her before this. Mary would be safe with her brothers, they were both big, strong lads. But she would be weary and bored and sick of the smelly corridor, too. Where was she?

Nell used the next little hitch forward in the line to hold back, creating enough space to turn around, bags and all. She rose up on her tiptoes, trying to see farther down the corridor. There was a sad parade of tired faces behind her. One old woman scowled at her and made a gesture, one finger pointed downward, circling. She wanted Nell to turn around.

"What are you doing?" Mama demanded.

"Trying to see Mary and her brothers."

Mama gripped her shoulder, forcing her around to face forward. "Keep your mind on your own. We may need you."

The line hitched forward again and Nell kept her eyes down, fighting tears. Weren't things frightening enough without Mama snipping at her for nothing at all?

The line moved twice more in little fits and starts, then began to ease forward steadily. Nell walked with short, careful steps, making sure she didn't step on the heels of the white-haired man. At the base of the stairway, Nell began to hear voices shouting overhead. In English? She wasn't sure. She couldn't make out what they were saying.

Just then, two men ahead of them in the line began shouting, their voices angry, and for a second she caught her breath. What would happen if someone decided to start a fight and came crashing down the stairs? But the voices subsided and the line moved on.

Granny Rose had a little trouble on the stairs and Nell took her arm.

"Get Fiona down," Mama said as they came closer to the lowered ceiling of the second tier of stairs. Patrick nodded.

"I know, Mama, I am just—"

"Get her down," Mama insisted.

Patrick let Fiona slide to one side, then held her tightly as he lowered her into his arms. She struggled, unhappy with the change.

"Patrick!" It was Granny Rose shouting and they all flinched, startled.

"What's wrong, Mother Dunne?" Mama asked as

she lifted her long skirt to continue up the steeper flight of stairs.

Granny bobbled to one side and she tried to answer, tripping on her own skirt.

"You have to pick up your hem, Granny Rose," Nell told her.

Granny Rose made a sound of disgust. "I do not need a child to tell me what to do with my skirts."

Nell swallowed hard. They all learned not to argue with Granny, but she had stopped. They had all stopped with her and the people behind them were already uneasy.

"Let's keep it moving," a man shouted and Nell looked up, startled. Somehow, they were alone at the head of the line now. There were fifteen or twenty steps above them, all empty. Nell could see a patch of gray sky behind the man who had shouted. He was leaning into the stairwell, gesturing at them.

"Mother Dunne, get hold of your skirts and let's do as the gentleman asks," Mama said.

Granny Rose shook her head without moving. "He is hardly a *gentleman*." She reached down to lift her skirts but did not move.

"Is there some trouble?" the man shouted down at them.

"No, sir," Patrick called back. In one quick motion, he handed Fiona to Nell and pulled Mama's bag from her shoulder. He ducked beneath the strap, motioning Nell to move forward. She shifted her own handful of hemline into her left hand and perched Fiona on her hip. Then she started upward, her legs aching from the hours they had stood waiting. Glancing back, she saw Patrick take Granny Rose's hand and guide her onto the next step, where she stopped again, glowering at him. "Where is Patrick?" she demanded. Nell went slowly, but kept moving. One step at a time her mother and Patrick persuaded Granny Rose up the stairs.

At the top, Nell stepped into the cold air and shivered. She felt Fiona shrink back against her chest, turning to keep the biting cold off her face. Nell dragged in a long breath and looked around. The clean, frigid air stung going into her lungs. She was the one who was supposed to take care of Granny Rose, not Patrick.

"Keep moving," the uniformed man said again. This time he sounded impatient and Nell hoped Granny Rose had not heard him. But, of course, she had.

"You seem to think that you can be rude to us, young man?" she accused. He did not answer and Mama and Patrick pulled Granny Rose forward. Nell looked around wildly.

"Down that ramp," the man said, jabbing a finger to indicate the direction. Nell saw a flash of white blond hair and realized how far they had fallen behind. It scared her.

"Walk as fast as you can, Granny Rose," she pleaded. "We have to get down there with the others."

Granny Rose looked at her sharply. "Do you see Patrick down there?"

Nell swallowed, flushing, angry with herself. Now she had aggravated her grandmother and things would only get worse. Nell sighed. If Granny Rose started demanding to see Granddad in front of the inspectors, what in the world would she do?

"I see Sean," Mama said suddenly. She looked up. "I see your da!"

For a split second, Nell thought she was fibbing, trying to distract Granny Rose from thinking that Granddad was somehow still alive and waiting for them. Then she turned and saw her mother's face. Mama's eyes were lit like winter windows and she was smiling, waving.

Holding Fiona tightly, Nell whirled around, scanning the dock below for her father. There were hundreds of men and all of them were waving, their arms above their heads.

"Where?" Nell demanded, turning to look at her mother.

"You have to move along," the man at the top of the stairs shouted. He was gesturing at them, clearly angry now.

Mama and Patrick took Granny Rose's arms and practically dragged her forward. Nell led the way, carrying Fiona on her hip. She nearly stumbled once because she could not take her eyes off the crowd of men on the dock, searching for her father's face. Once on the ramp, she had to stop to slide the strap of her mother's bag higher on her shoulder. No one minded. The ramp was wide enough that the people behind them just went around.

Granny Rose took advantage of the pause to look over the railing. "I don't see Sean!" she said in a low voice. "Where's my son?" She didn't sound angry anymore, she sounded scared.

"There!" Mama said, pointing.

Fiona began to whimper and Nell held her tighter.

"Oh, sweet God, it is him," Granny Rose said and her voice was unsteady. Nell followed her mother's gesture. People from the ship streamed past them, nearly everyone looking downward to the dock.

"I see him, too!" Patrick whooped suddenly. He stood close behind Nell and pointed, leaning over her shoulder so she could sight down his arm. Fiona laughed and grabbed at his hand and held it down. He pulled free and pointed again. "There, Nell, see him?"

In one shivering instant, Nell spotted her father and felt her heart swell with joy. Da was grinning. He lifted his hat and threw his arms wide. Patrick moved to stand behind Granny Rose. "There," Nell heard him say. "He's just in front of the man with the gray fur hat."

After a few seconds, Granny Rose murmured something Nell couldn't understand, but the expression on her face was clear as rainwater. She began waving. "Let's go then," she said happily. She lifted her skirts and started up the ramp, but Patrick quickly hooked his arm through hers and walked a tiny circle, turning her around like a man with a dance partner. If Granny Rose noticed the maneuver, she didn't say anything. Nell started downward, glancing off to the right to smile at her father every few seconds.

At the bottom of the ramp, Granny Rose tried to turn to her right.

"You can't go this way, Ma'am." The stern voice belonged to another man in uniform. He had a bristling black beard and red cheeks. "Ellis Island first."

Nell remembered now what her brother had told them earlier and she felt her heart shrink.

"Remember what Sean told us in the letter?" Mama was explaining fast, trying hard to make Granny walk without stopping. "We have to go out to Ellis Island before we can go with him to our new home. We have to show our papers and so on and—"

"Look at that!" Patrick said, turning back to catch Nell's eye. He pointed and she looked off to the left. Out in the harbor was the famous statue. They had been told about it—the whole world had heard of the Statue of Liberty. It was remarkably beautiful,

Nell thought, the figure's robes hanging with a grace that seemed impossible. Nell's eyes drifted from the statue to the flat little island to the right of the Lady of Liberty. Ellis Island? There was another, much bigger, to the left. Nell swallowed nervously, then she looked back at the city rising from the water before them. The buildings were so tall it took her breath away.

"Are those mountains?" Granny Rose asked.

"That's New York City," Patrick told her.

Nell stared. It looked like a fairy dwelling. The day was gloomy enough for people to have their lights still lit. There were thousands of windows glowing warm amber or shining white. Nell wondered what sort of lamp burned pure white like that. It looked like magic to her.

"Move along, please," the man with the beard said firmly, interrupting her thoughts.

Almost stumbling, again fighting to manage her little sister, her bag, and her skirts, Nell followed her family down the snow-dusted pier.

CHAPTER SIX

Nell stared in disbelief as they got closer. The wharf had what looked like cattle pens built on it. The uniformed men were directing people *inside* the pens.

"How long will we be here?" Mama asked the man who was waving them along. Her voice was strained.

"No way to know, lady," he answered her in a polite tone. But when Mama opened her mouth to ask another question he frowned and shrugged, a final, resolute gesture as he motioned for them to keep moving.

"Nell?" Mama turned.

Nell lifted her chin. "Yes?"

"Give me your sister."

Nell handed Fiona to Mama. Fiona, always delighted to go back to the arms she loved the best, began to pluck at Mama's blouse. "She's hungry," Mama said aloud. There was a hopelessness in her voice and Nell knew what she was thinking. How in the world could she nurse Fiona in this crowd? It was impossible. And the hard breads that Mama and Granny Rose had brought from home were long gone.

"That way, please." A gruff voice startled them from their right-hand side. Nell turned to see another uniform. The man wearing it was tall and very thin. He wore gloves and a fur hat pulled low over his ears. "That way," he repeated, and there was no emotion at all in his voice. He might have been talking to himself.

Patrick turned and stared back down the pier. Nell turned with him, hoping to catch another glimpse of their father, but there was a straggling parade of people behind them, blocking their view. Nell sighed. Her shoulders hurt from the weight of the bags and from carrying Fiona.

"I'm cold," Granny Rose said aloud.

Mama said something soothing and Patrick just grunted as he shrugged the bags higher on his shoulders.

"Let's go," he said.

Nell nodded. There really was nothing else they could do. She looked out across the water of the bay, then back toward the city. Those buildings cannot be real, she thought. How in the world could anyone build anything that tall and have it stand in a wind?

"Nell!" Mama said sharply. She turned and nearly bumped into a woman wearing a dark scarf pulled so close that it was impossible to see her face.

Mumbling an apology, Nell hurried to catch up with her family. Granny Rose had her arm through Patrick's. Mama's arms were full of a wriggling Fiona. Nell hurried to take Granny Rose's free hand. With Mama leading the way, they walked through the gate of the cattle pen and joined the crowds inside.

"Take a place in the middle somewhere," Patrick said in a low voice.

Nell looked up at him over Granny Rose's head. "Why?"

"Warmer," Mama answered over her shoulder, and Nell understood instantly. She veered a little, aiming for the center of the fenced enclosure, the snow squeaking between her shoe soles and the planks of the dock. Near the far side, she caught a glimpse of too white hair and saw the blue-eyed man sitting on the cold planks, his arms around his knees, his head down.

Without saying another word, they found a place toward the center of the enclosure. Moving stiffly, Nell followed Patrick's lead and they set their bags down on the frost-crusted planks, then sat down on them. Nell and Granny Rose shared Mama's bag. Mama held Fiona and she and Patrick sat with their backs toward Nell and Granny Rose. They moved closer together by inches, until they were leaning against each other, sheltering each other from the wind that stole the warmth from beneath their coats.

It was still impossible to stay warm. Nell exhaled slowly, watching her breath curl in the early morning air. The people who came behind them straggled into the enclosures in ones and twos, finding places to sit. Some of the bigger families took a little time to get settled, parents calling after their children in a dozen languages. One of Patrick's friends from the ship came to talk with him for a minute, then went back to stand with his father near the railing. Nell kept watching the new faces as they came closer, but she couldn't spot Mary or her brothers. Maybe they had been closer to the front of the line. If so, they were probably in one of the pens farther down the dock.

Nell scanned the faces she could see, but she was too tired and too cold to stand up and walk around—and too scared. The city loomed so close, and as much as she had hated being on the ship, she found herself almost wanting to run back up the ramp. New York City seemed too big, too strange.

"There it is," Patrick said after a long silence. He pointed. "Do you see it? The island."

Nell turned and stared. "Ellis Island?"

Patrick nodded. "It has to be. See the towers? And it isn't too far off the shore over there."

Nell nodded. The building looked almost as much like a fairy house as the improbable city of New York did. She shivered. How could people be expected to sit in the middle of a snow-cold morning out in the open like this? A deafening blast of a ship's whistle startled her into half standing, her heart pounding like a rabbit's. Angry with herself, she sat down again, apologizing to Granny Rose for jostling her.

"It scared me," Nell mumbled when Patrick made a sound of disapproval. She bit at the inside of her lip, sitting hunched over. After a few minutes she worked her hands up inside her sleeves, crossing her arms over her chest. Fiona cried for a while because she could not nurse, and then finally fell asleep in Mama's arms. Granny Rose leaned back against Patrick's shoulder and closed her eyes. After a time she began to snore.

Nell stared out over the water. The harbor around them was alive with ships and ferryboats, all shoving their way through the freezing gray water. Nell watched them closely at first, waiting to see which one would come their way, which one would take them to the tiny island where everything would go right—or wrong. But none of the boats slowed, none turned toward them. It was as though, in the bustle of the city, they were invisible, unimportant.

The people around them quieted and dozed, with only the cries of too-cold children to break the rhythmic slapping of the waves against the dock. Nell kept turning as far as she could without disturbing Granny Rose, first to stare at Ellis Island across the bay, then to look back at the city. Both made her uneasy.

"Where do you suppose your father will wait?" Mama said in a low voice, and Nell knew she was talking quietly to keep from waking Fiona.

"I don't know, Mama," she answered softly.

Mama was rocking a little to keep Fiona from waking up. "I am so grateful that we got to see him." She sniffled and Nell twisted around to see her mother use the corner of her scarf to dab at her eyes.

"He looks the same," Patrick murmured.

Mama sniffed. "That he does. Handsome and dear."

Nell smiled a little and shut her eyes. She listened to the soft voices all around them and the sounds of the ships passing. She tried hard to doze off, but she couldn't. Granny Rose's steady, soft snoring was as familiar as anything else in Nell's life and it was a comfort as she opened her eyes and looked out over the cold gray water again.

The wind rose a little at a time—so slowly that it was barely noticeable at first. Nell shivered, crossing her arms tighter across her chest. "It's getting colder," she said quietly, not sure whether her mother or Patrick were awake.

"I want to get Patrick's old jacket out of my bag," Mama said, nudging her.

Nell turned. "Wake Granny Rose?"

"We have to. I am afraid for Fiona in this weather."

Nell stood and gently shook Granny Rose. She opened her eyes at once. She looked so startled, so completely confused, that Nell bent to kiss her cheek. "Mama has to get an extra jacket to wrap Fiona in."

Granny Rose stared at her without answering.

"We are sitting on the bag," Nell added. Granny Rose looked away from her, out across the water. Nell realized what was wrong. The nap had been like a night's sleep for her, and she was confused.

"We're just waiting for a ferryboat to come to take us to Ellis Island," Nell explained, trying to smile.

Granny Rose frowned. "We are here in America, Granny Rose," Patrick said suddenly, and a little too loudly. "You saw Da, remember?"

Granny Rose's face came into focus and she nodded. "He looked well."

"We need to get into the bag you are sitting on," Nell said quickly. "We need you to stand up a minute."

Granny Rose struggled to her feet, stiff kneed in the cold. Patrick stood to brace her up as she stood, swaying on her feet. Nell undid the buckles as quickly as she could, her teeth chattering.

"Get a pair of woolies out, too," Mama said as Nell handed her the jacket.

Without asking why, Nell bent back over the bag. When she straightened up, Mama took the heavy knit socks from her in one quick motion. Fiona was whimpering now.

Nell closed the bag and sat again as Mama pulled the adult-size socks up over Fiona's shoes. They covered her legs completely. Working swiftly, Mama straightened Fiona's dress, then wrapped her in the extra jacket, using the collar as a loose hood, turning it down to cover Fiona's forehead and ears, the sleeves tied across her chest.

Granny Rose settled back down. Patrick stretched and stamped his feet for a full minute before he sank to the bag again. Mama was humming, a tuneless, hopeless little melody that made Nell's heart ache. What must Da be thinking? He couldn't help them. Couldn't even come near enough to shout encouragement. No one's family could, she was sure, or they would have by now.

Nell wrenched around to look back up the dock. The crowd had cleared as far as she could see. The *Astoria* was still moored there, towering white and cold above the planked dock, but the ramp was empty now. And no one stood near the rail on the decks above. The dock beside the ship was cleared as well.

Maybe the men in uniform had made Da and the others move along, too. But to where? How would they find Da again when they came back from Ellis Island? Without meaning to, she turned and looked back at the incredible buildings. They were uneven, different shades of brown in the muted light. She glanced up at the sky. The clouds were thick.

At that moment it began to snow again. The white flakes fell at a slant, driven by the wind. They struck Nell's cheeks and stung. Granny Rose huddled lower, hiding her face in Patrick's jacket. He put his arms around her, ducking his own chin to keep the snow from pelting him.

Someone began sobbing, a choking, rending sound. Nell pulled her hands from her sleeves and put her fingers in her ears against the horrible sound.

CHAPTER SEVEN

The snow muted everything, even the sound of the crying. Nell took her icy fingers from her ears after a few minutes and tucked her hands back up inside her sleeves, crossing her arms over her chest again. The wind swirled the heavy flakes and as it eased, the snow seemed to get bigger and bigger. The flakes dotted her dark wool coat and she stared at them.

The shapes were exquisite—like nothing she had ever seen. She had seen snow at home once or twice, but it was always muddy stuff, dissolved by cold rain in a few days at most. This snow was like fairy snow. The flakes were as big as her thumbnail, and intricately shaped. Against the black wool of her sleeve, they seemed dreamlike, as impossible as the buildings that she knew still towered somewhere behind her. She half thought about turning to look at them once more, but it seemed like too much trouble. The silence on the dock was unbroken now except for the slapping of the waves against the wood planks. It was wonderful. Comfortable.

"Get up," Patrick said suddenly, too loudly, too close to her ear. She blinked and realized that her eyes had been closed. She didn't remember closing them.

"Get up and jump up and down," Patrick commanded.

Nell got to her feet, fighting tears. He was right, she knew it. She was freezing and she had to warm up. But it all seemed too hard. She was so tired.

"Up, Mama," Patrick was shouting—or at least it seemed like he was shouting. Nell tugged at her mother's sleeve and they rose together.

"What's all your fussing about?" Granny Rose asked irritably when Nell turned to pull at her coat. Patrick helped and they got her to her feet. For a minute or so, all they could do was tramp their feet in place, barely bending their knees. "Come, Granny Rose," Nell pleaded when she saw her grandmother stand still again. "We have to get warm."

"There's too much wind," Granny Rose complained. "Patrick should be here by now."

Nell nodded to let her grandmother know she had heard, but she didn't answer. The truth was she had no will to argue, or even to comfort Granny Rose. It was all she could do to make herself keep moving. Fiona woke and cried thinly, her wail scarcely carrying.

The wind whistled along the edge of the dock, picking up a fine mist of sea spray that made it even colder. "Keep moving," Patrick said, reaching out to grip her shoulder. Nell nodded and he turned back to Granny Rose and leaned down to cajole her, talking earnestly into her ear. Turning away from the next hissing gust of sea wind, she saw her mother bent over Fiona, shielding her with her body.

A sudden jab of anger went through Nell and she had no idea who or what she was angry with. Her father had certainly never intended for them to freeze to death on the New York docks. Nor was the storm to blame. It was a force of nature, of God, and who knew the reasons for things like storms? The shipowners? Was this their fault? Even though she had no one to blame for her misery, the anger stayed, curled up in her stomach, and in an odd way, it warmed the rest of her. She began stamping her numb feet, swaying back and forth and squeezing her hands into fists. All around them people began to rouse themselves. In minutes there was motion on every side of them. People stood, stretched, and began marching back and forth, walking with their heads down and their eyes slit against the wind.

Nell didn't even look up at the sound of a ship's horn. It was close, but a lot of boats had come close, then sailed straight past. It wasn't until Patrick grabbed her shoulder and turned her seaward that she saw that the ferry was coming in, swinging sideward so that the gates faced the dock.

Nell stared at the odd-looking ferry. It was open, unroofed, and the white-slatted railing made it look as much like an animal pen as the enclosures they had been herded into on the dock.

"This is an Ellis Island ferry," a man shouted out, and Nell saw one of the dark uniforms she had gotten used to on the ship. This man had a scarf wound around his neck and covering half his face. Where had he been? He hadn't been down on the dock with them, of that much she was sure. Maybe he had been watching from the *Astoria*. The anger in her stomach swelled and she tightened her hands. How could anyone sit in a warm ship's cabin and watch them freezing like animals left out in the storm?

"Let's go!" the man shouted.

Patrick was helping Granny Rose stretch her cramped knees. Mama was struggling to get her bag over her shoulder.

"I'll get it, Mama," Nell told her. "Or Patrick will."

"I can take that one," Patrick said, "Nell, can you help Granny Rose?"

Mama nodded, and then she turned. "Mother Dunne? Can you walk?"

"Yes," Granny Rose said firmly. "I can."

Nell squared her shoulders. If her Grandmother

could sound that strong and sure, so could she. She glanced at the barge, trying to think as Patrick had, about what would be best for them all. "Maybe we should hold back," she said aloud.

"Why?" Patrick asked.

"Last on, first off."

"Good girl," Mama said. "The Dunnes aren't so easily defeated. You have your father's good brain."

Nell stood a little taller. Patrick shot her a smile, then turned his attention back to Granny Rose. She'd said she could walk, but it wasn't entirely true. She was leaning heavily on his arm. Nell went to help.

"Quickly now, move along!" The shout came from farther down the dock.

As people began to move toward the barge, Nell heard a rumbling sound, like heavy boards being dragged along. Then there was a dull heavy thudding sound.

"Step right onto the ramps, please," the uniformed man shouted now. He repeated it three or four times, each shout getting louder as he worked his way back toward them.

"Don't push," the man hollered at someone Nell couldn't see. "If you can't all fit here, there's another barge coming along soon."

Nell's stomach tightened. *Soon.* The word sounded ugly and uncertain. Another hour in the cold was more than she could bear—and what about Fiona and Granny Rose? "We don't want to get left here," she said aloud.

Mama nodded. "Two-thirds of these can't speak English. Just work your way forward, Nell. We will follow you."

Nell settled the bagstrap on her shoulder and let go of Granny Rose's hand. Patrick would steady her. Nell led off, moving slowly but steadily forward. The crowd was eager to be off the dock, too, no matter what they had understood or not understood, and it wasn't easy to find a way through them. But some were fiddling with their bundles or arguing with each other or were just too polite to wedge their way between those moving more slowly. Nell tried to take advantage of every gap, every small space between groups of people. Her family stayed close on her heels.

Glancing back every few seconds to make sure that Mama was keeping up and that Patrick and Granny weren't far behind, Nell worked her way along the rail fence until she came to an unopened gate. She stared at the latch. It wasn't locked. But the uniformed man had only opened the gate nearest the ferry. Nell looked across the fence. No one was walking there—the slim strip of the dock just outside the fence was empty.

Nell paused and looked back, waiting for Mama to come close. The she pointed at the gate, raising her eyebrows. At first Mama seemed not to understand, but then she came forward and flipped the latch open herself. Nell led the way through and Patrick closed it behind himself, Nell saw. She looked back to see if anyone had noticed, if the uniformed man was going to run up, shouting at them. Then she faced forward and walked as fast as she dared, staying close to the railing.

The ferry's ramp was crowded; an unending stream of people was spilling through the gate the uniformed man *had* opened. Nell looked at them in despair. Who would let them in line? Maybe she had been very foolish trying to outwit the others.

"And where have you been?"

The familiar voice, laden with an unfamiliar accent, made Nell look up. Mary was grinning, her teeth chattering. And she was holding out her arms to stop her brothers, one on each side of her. Together they made a human fence, stopping the flow of people just long enough to let Nell and her family get onto the ramp.

CHAPTER EIGHT

"I've been looking for you," Mary said as the ferry's whistle blew sharply, three times.

Nell smiled and shivered, her whole body shuddering.

"We thought we might get left back," Patrick was explaining to Mary's oldest brother. "Or my sister did," he corrected himself when she shot him a glance. "We were pretty far up on the dock."

"That's it," someone yelled, and there was an answer that Nell couldn't understand. Then more shouting started and she heard the scraping of heavy wood again. They were dragging the ramp back.

"She was right," Mary's brother said. Nell realized that she didn't know which was Will and which Angus. She had been around them two or three times for a few moments each time. They had mostly been off, like Patrick, with boys their own age. To make it harder, they looked a great deal alike, both tall with light hair that curled in ringlets.

"Too bad our sister is not half so smart," the taller one said.

Mary pinched Nell and winked. "Angus doesn't mean that."

"Oh, but I do," Angus answered.

"Enough," Mama said, and they all quieted. Then she sighed. "I wish there were benches," she said and the boys all shuffled their feet, embarrassed to have been teasing.

"I could carry Fiona now, Mama," Patrick offered.

Mama sighed and nodded. "You must button her up inside your coat, though," she said. "Patrick, she has to be kept warm."

"I will," Patrick said somberly, and Nell knew he was remembering Da's letter and his stern instructions. Nell faced her grandmother, sliding the bag off her shoulder as she turned. "Do you want to sit on the bag, Granny Rose?"

"I would like to sit anywhere." Granny Rose smiled a little and patted Nell's cheek with an ice-cold hand. Nell set the bag down and Granny Rose and Mama both stepped near to it and prepared to settle themselves.

"Oh, dear God," Mama said suddenly. When Nell glanced at her she pointed.

Nell looked back toward the dock as the ferry

slid past it. Three of the uniformed men were standing in a little knot. They were bent over someone lying flat on the snow-crusted plank. Nell caught a glimpse of white blond hair.

"He's dead, I think," Mama said quietly.

"Oh, no," Nell breathed. Her heart beat hard inside her chest. It wasn't possible. She had stood next to him all those terrible hours in the ship's corridor. She had noticed him on the dock. She had looked right at him as he'd taken his place at the edge of the crowd.

"He was alone," Patrick said flatly.

Mama murmured an assent. Nell turned away, tears stinging at her eyes. The man had been alone. He had had no one to help him stay warm, no one to tell him to stand up and move around before he froze. He had come to America alone and died alone.

"He was nice," Mary said.

Nell nodded. "He was."

"You don't know what he was or wasn't," Will said, mocking Mary's somber tone.

Mary's eyes flashed with anger. "He gave me part of his bread one evening. He talked to me about his wife. She died a year ago so he decided to come here to get away from memories of her."

No one answered and Nell remembered seeing the man on the dock. Why hadn't she thought about him being alone? It would have been easy to invite him to join them. If they had, he would probably still be alive. A hollowness inside her opened up, and her eyes flooded with tears. Mama had more or less insulted him when he had spoken to her. And now he was dead.

"There, there," Will said, reaching across to pat Nell's head. "Mary, look what you've done. As though we don't all have enough sadness of our own."

"She didn't mean to upset me," Nell defended Mary and got a quick smile in return.

"She doesn't think, our sister," Will taunted. "Unlike Patrick's."

"Enough," Mama said, and they all hushed a second time.

As Mama and Granny Rose sat down and Patrick and Mary's brothers worked out an arrangement for themselves, Nell stepped to the rail and looked out across the widening band of gray water that separated them from the dock.

"Did anyone even know his name?" she asked softly.

Mary heard and came closer to stand beside her. "The ship's manifest would have it. If he ever told me, I can't remember it."

"You talked to him about his wife?" Nell asked her.

Mary nodded. "I talk to everyone about everything. It will make me a better actress, my uncle says."

For a long second Nell hesitated. Then she decided to say what was in her heart. "I saw my father," Nell said slowly, looking into Mary's face. She didn't want to be cruel. After all, Mary's parents were both dead.

There was a shadow of sorrow in Mary's eyes, but it passed in an instant and she smiled. "That is pure joy and wonderful."

Nell smiled back. "I would like to stay friends."

Mary put out her hand. "I would, too. No matter what."

Nell took her hand and shook it, imitating the men she had known in her life. She had never seen women shake hands before. How like Mary it was to do something like this—something other girls didn't do.

The wind was getting stronger as the ferry's engines chugged, dragging them away from the dock, out through the choppy water. It felt odd to be going back the way they had come. It felt wrong.

Nell was so tired. Her knees were weak, but she didn't want to sit down. Not now. Chugging back across the river's mouth they had passed coming into the harbor, she watched the skyline of the city drift past.

"Have you ever seen buildings that big in your life?" Mary asked. "Or dreamed that there could be such a thing?"

Nell shook her head. "Liverpool has big ones but nothing near so tall."

"Nor any city I've seen, which is two, counting this one." Mary laughed.

Nell nodded. "Until we left to come here, I went to market with my mother once a month or so, never anywhere else."

"And now look at us," Mary said, laughing. "World voyagers, sure enough. We will remember this until . . . "

Mary hesitated and Nell turned to look at her. "Until we die," Nell finished for her. "And maybe beyond."

Mary nodded and all the mischief in her face had faded into a somber expression. "That we will," she said, sounding Irish as anyone ever had. She put out her hand again and Nell took it. Then, holding hands, they turned to face the water again. Ellis Island was getting bigger. Nell could see the odd spires on the big building more clearly now.

"I will remember you forever, too," Mary said suddenly. Nell squeezed her hand, understanding why she had said it. There, on the flat little island that barely rose out of the gray water of the huge bay, their lives in America would begin. In a strange way, it was like being born on the same day, and sharing it with someone.

Nell scanned the faces of the people closest to

them on the ferry. They all looked weary. They were hunched against the bite of the wind, and yet their eyes were alive with hope. As she looked at them she felt their images being set in her mind and her heart, and she knew that even though she had never spoken a single word to most of them, in some way they were all now connected. She knew that she would remember their faces later in her life. She would remember the wind and the blond man and even the way the snow smelled, the huge lacy flakes on her sleeve. This day, whether it ended in joy or sadness, would be with her all her life.

"Look." Mary breathed and Nell turned back. They were getting closer to Ellis Island now. The big building looked like a castle, a palace, the home of some great lord.

CHAPTER NINE

The ferry pulled closer to the island and Nell saw a long dock that stretched in front of the building, with rails built at intervals along it. There were already two ferries there. One still had people aboard. In front of the building was a long covered walkway. Beneath it, people milled around, some of them talking and laughing.

The ferry engines stopped and Nell realized how loud they had been because of the hollow silence they left behind. The sudden hush seemed odd, out of place. Nell realized that she could hear people talking all around her again. She glanced back. Patrick had already helped Mama up, and Angus and Will were getting Granny Rose to her feet. She was grateful to them.

The building was huge, made of red brick that looked impossibly dark against the snow-covered grounds around it. Nell squinted, blinking away the wind tears to see more clearly. There were two sculptures of eagles, their stone faces sharp and angry, their talons clutching stone shields.

"Here we are," Mary whispered, bending close to her ear.

Nell nodded but didn't answer. Her stomach was tightening again. The building had a thousand windows, at least, clustered together into arched shapes. Three of these massive arches were centered at the end of the roofed walkway. The lights inside were bright white, shining even in the gloomy light of this cloudy day. They were the same clear colorless lights she had seen from the dock. Electric lights, she realized suddenly. She had heard of them. At the corners of the main structure were beautiful rounded towers sheathed in dark brown metal. It was probably copper, Nell decided, though it looked too dark in the bleak light.

"It's so beautiful," Mary whispered. Nell nodded and swallowed hard. It was. But it was so *big*. She had never been inside a building this big. She had never seen one.

"Wait until the ferry has come to a complete stop," a man was shouting. "Stay where you are."

Nell spotted him. He wasn't on the ferry, but stood on the dock, walking the length of the boat. He was holding up one hand, his palm toward them in a gesture that would be hard to misunderstand even for those who spoke no English. He shouted his order again, then once more after he had passed them and was facing the bow end of the ferry.

"Oh, dear God," Mama said. "I hope we don't have to wait anymore."

"I can't feel my feet," Granny Rose said. She began to stamp, marching in place as they had done on the first dock. Nell looked at the huge building and the crowds in front of it and pulled in a deep breath.

"I wish your father could have come with us," Mama murmured. "That I wish with all my heart."

Nell nodded again. Her father had been through all this once. He wouldn't be scared.

"Stop worrying," Mary said, nudging her.

Nell nodded once more, still afraid to trust her voice. Mary squeezed her hand.

"Oh, no!" Patrick smacked his hand on the guardrail, frowning. Then he sighed. "They were here first."

Nell looked up and followed his gaze. The ferry in front of them was lowering a ramp. The uniformed men worked quickly, dragging it into place. A few seconds later, people began to shuffle down it. They all moved stiffly, as though their bodies were half frozen.

Nell watched them, transfixed by their silence and the fear on their faces as they came back toward the main walkway, passing within fifteen feet of where she stood.

"We look like that," Mary whispered, and Nell turned to meet her eyes. "Raggy and tired," Mary said slowly. "Scared and hungry."

Nell looked back at the people passing in front of them and knew Mary was right. A man in long, flowing white robes crossed in front of them. His wife wore a hooded robe that came up over her head and hid her face completely.

"Not so bad today," Nell heard Patrick say. "But summers here are hot, Da says. I don't envy her then. Do you have all the papers close to hand, Mama?"

For an answer, Mama patted the pocket of her heavy coat and Patrick said no more.

"Do you have ours?" Mary asked Angus.

He smiled. "And who else's would I have?"

Mary poked at him halfheartedly. "This isn't funny, Angus. And you beware, please. None of your sharp-tongued anarchy talk for the inspectors."

"I am not afraid of them," Angus said flatly.

"But Angus, you be careful, that's all. There's too much at risk," Mary argued.

"I am not afraid. Neither am I stupid, little sister," Angus said.

Mary made an angry sound but said no more. She turned back to face the slow parade of people passing them by. Nell stepped closer to her, standing so that their shoulders touched. She heard her mother make a little sound of dismay from behind them, but ignored her. Mama might be right about Mary not having the best manners, but she had a very good heart.

Stamping her feet to try to pound feeling back into them, Nell wondered at herself. She was feeling passing strange. Usually, the idea of Mama being angry with her was enough to stop her at most anything. But standing here shivering in the freezing air, staring at the enormous redbrick building before her, Mama being angry seemed less like the end of the world.

Nell glanced back at Granny Rose. She stood erect, still marching, fighting to stay warm. Patrick and Mary's brothers were lost in talking in low voices, and they had drawn off a little to one side.

"I hope we don't have to wait much longer," Mary whispered.

Nell turned back around. The last of the people from the ferry in front of them were straggling past. One old man was limping and half dragging his bag behind him. He seemed to be with a woman and her three little children. Her father? An old uncle? The woman and all the children wore oddly tight-fitting coats and high shiny black shoes.

"I wonder if they will let the old man in?" Nell said quietly, assuming that the family did not speak English.

The woman turned to glare at her, an expression of hateful reprove on her face.

"Oh, I am sorry," Nell began, but of course it was too late, they had already passed by. She watched, feeling dismal, as the woman gathered her children close and they entered the edge of the crowds.

"What are all those people doing?" Mama asked. "Not the ones like us. The other ones."

"Which ones?" Nell was confused.

"Watch," Mama said.

Nell tried to follow the progress of the woman and her old father through the crowds outside the grand doors to the redbrick building. At first, she couldn't see what her mother was talking about. But then, after a moment, she noticed that some of the people were not moving toward the double doors at all. They were standing still, leaning out toward the stream of people moving past, shouting and talking.

"Like flies," Mama said. "Those are not honest men."

"You don't know what they are, Mama," Patrick said incredulously. "How can you tell from here what kind of—"

A sudden spate of shouting hushed him. Nell stared, scanning the crowds for the source of the yelling. Two men, one tall and dark-skinned, the other small and very pale, were squaring off as though they were about to fight. They were shouting in a language

Nell could not understand, but their anger was very clear. A ring of people formed, watching the confrontation.

A man in a uniform stepped closer and the small pale-skinned man seemed to see him first. He reached into his pocket and handed something to the taller man. The shouting died down, and before the uniformed man could get too close, Nell saw the paler man dodge his way through the ring of watchers, running a few steps then slowing down.

The tall man stood still a moment, then he waved the paper the pale man had given him over his head. A woman's voice called out in excitement. The tall man laughed, shaking his head, and started back toward her.

"What do you suppose that was about?" Mary breathed.

There was a murmur among the people on the ferry and Nell knew they had not been the only ones to watch the scene and wonder what had happened. She shook her head. "Just some argument. People are so tired, so cold."

Mary sighed. "Now I'm the one worrying."

Nell smiled. She stamped her feet faster. How long could they be left out in the weather like this? Didn't anyone care how miserable they were?

"I really liked that man," Mary said softly, and Nell knew at once who she was talking about.

"I did, too," she answered, in a voice so low that no one but Mary could hear. She pictured the white-haired man again, hunched over alone on the dock, freezing to death, and no one had even noticed. She hadn't.

Someone behind them began to weep and Nell turned, afraid it was her mother, but it wasn't. Mama and Granny Rose had sat back down. Fiona was snuggled against Mama's chest, just her head, hooded by the jacket, sticking out of Mama's coat collar. Granny Rose had closed her eyes. It scared Nell. What if they had to wait another hour or two or even longer?

Feeling helpless, her heart aching, Nell turned back to look at the huge, redbrick building again. It was as though the whole world was as vague and gray as the sky and only that monstrous building was real, heavy and solid.

A sharp, scraping sound startled Nell into opening her eyes. She was leaning on Mary, who had fallen asleep—slumped against her brother Will. Nell blinked, confused. She didn't remember sitting down or deciding to try to sleep. How long had she been dozing? The scraping sound came again, this time with a shout.

"Folks?" came a man's voice. "Time to go in!"

Nell tried to stand quickly, but her legs were

cramped and her knees were stiff from sitting with her feet tucked beneath her for warmth. She very nearly fell. Mary grabbed at her as she staggered to her own feet.

Nell turned. Fiona and Mama were both awake now, Fiona crying softly as Mama blinked. Mama was reaching for Patrick's hand. Granny Rose's eyes were still closed.

"Granny Rose?" Nell called, and her voice was as stiff and graceless as the rest of her body. "Granny Rose!" There was no stirring of Granny Rose's wrinkled eyelids. She did not move at all.

Fear gripped Nell's heart and she stumbled forward, then bent over her grandmother, pulling at her coat. "Granny Rose?"

There was a terrible pause, but then Granny Rose opened her eyes. She had that lost, unfocused look on her face and Nell bent close to her ear. "We are waiting to go in to the inspectors, Granny Rose. They've just called us."

"Inspectors? Inspecting what?"

"The Americans," Mama said smoothly, coming to help Granny Rose to her feet. Nell took her grandmother's right hand while her mother pulled at her left. Granny Rose managed to stand.

"After all that time on the ship, we have finally arrived," Mama was saying in a calm voice. "And in a few hours, when they are done with us, we can go find Sean."

The sound of her son's name seemed to make everything else fall into place and Granny Rose nodded. "We should get started then." Granny Rose had always said that hard work ended faster if it was started sooner. She sounded like herself, like the no-nonsense woman Nell had known all her life.

"Mama?" Patrick began, turning toward her. "Are you ready?"

Mama took a deep breath. "I am. And you, Nell?"

Nell nodded. "Yes."

But it was Granny Rose who turned first to head toward the ramp. Nell hurried to stay close, ready to help her grandmother if she slipped on the slick, snowy deck.

CHAPTER TEN

The people all walked slowly, crippled by the cold. Nell saw men in uniforms standing back on both sides, watching them as they passed from the paving stones of the dock onto the walkway. Mary and her brothers were just behind them, and Nell kept glancing back at them. For all their brave talk, all three looked scared. Nell tried to catch Mary's eye to smile at her, but she was looking upward mostly, at the grand facade of the building.

And it *was* grand. The copper-clad towers were rounded, like nothing she had ever seen. They had rods sticking straight up from them, too, as though the builder had wanted to poke God in the eye. The window-filled arches across the front seemed as wide as a field.

The line stopped and Nell nearly ran into her mother from behind. A uniformed man was standing there. He spoke in a terse growl, and Nell could see him shivering. "Papers?"

Mama opened her coat and handed Fiona to Nell. She was still warm and sleepy and Nell was grateful. She unbuttoned her own coat and held Fiona against her chest as Mama handed the men the papers they had been issued when they boarded the *Astoria*. Nell could see how nervous her mother was. Mama's hands were shaking and her voice was thin and unsure.

"You are coming from England?" the man demanded brusquely.

"From Ireland," Mama told him.

He flipped over the paper he was looking at, then turned it back. "From Ireland?"

Mama cleared her throat. "We went first to Liverpool. I've a cousin there and thought I might not see her again for a long—"

"So you are from Ireland but got on the ship in Liverpool?" the man asked, cutting her off.

Mama nodded.

Abruptly, the man opened a case and bent over it for a moment. When he straightened, he had something in his hand. Before Nell could react, he was pinning a tag to her coat. "Don't remove these until you are processed completely," he said to her. "Understand?" Nell nodded. He slowed, poised over her with another tag. "Open your coat, please," he said after an awkward few seconds.

Finally, Nell understood. She was so used to carrying Fiona that if her sister was asleep—and still and quiet—she almost forgot about her. Nell freed one hand and pulled her coat open. The inspector pinned a tag on Fiona's back and stepped away. He turned to Mama, pausing only a split second before he jabbed a pin through the cloth of her coat, fixing the tag perfectly. Then he faced Patrick, who stepped forward eagerly. Granny Rose tried to push the man away, but he was so practiced with the pins that he had the tag on her lapel before she could do more than lift her hands.

"Go on in now," the man said loudly. "Step along, please." He was already looking past them, motioning the next family to come forward. He nudged Granny Rose as she passed him and she swung her fist in an arc that narrowly missed the side of his head. He seemed not to notice. He was already looking through his pile of papers, talking to the family behind them.

Mama walked a little ways, then stopped and glanced at Nell before reaching out to take Fiona back again. As Nell handed her sleeping sister back to Mama, she leaned closer. "Stay with your grandmother."

"I will," Nell promised.

"Lady?"

It was a short, heavyset man with a bushy gray-and-black beard. He was talking urgently as he hurried toward them, glancing back and forth as he came. Mama looked up, then to one side.

"Lady? I'm just waiting here for my wife. If you would like help with your luggage, I can carry something for you. I—"

He broke off as he seemed to see Nell for the first time. "You poor little thing. That must be terribly heavy for you. Let me just—" He extended his hand and Nell almost leaned toward him. The idea of not having to carry the heavy bag that dragged at her aching shoulder was almost too good to be true.

"Nell!" Mama said sharply.

Nell looked down at her scuffed shoes. Of course. Mama wouldn't let her talk to a stranger, so she would have to carry the bag the whole way instead of getting help. "Mama? It really is heavy," she began, but Mama shot her a look so fierce that she closed her mouth. She looked back toward the bearded man in time to see him scowl and turn to the next unescorted woman in the crowd. She clutched her bag tighter and hurried past him, looking annoyed.

Nell was amazed and puzzled. The man didn't seem daunted in the least. He just hung back a moment and let a few people pass by, then approached another woman. This one gratefully handed him her bag. He spun on his heel and began walking away with it. The woman shouted, then screamed. Nell blinked, understanding at last. The man was a thief.

"Move a little faster, please," a man in a uniform was saying. Nell looked forward in time to see the ferocious-looking eagles glaring down at them. Then they passed beneath the roof that spanned the walkway. It was glass, she realized, supported by an intricate iron structure. It was beautiful beneath it, sheltered, but the daylight barely dimmed.

"Will you need a ferry ticket going back?" a man asked kindly, approaching Mama. She glared at him. He immediately sidestepped to let her pass, and Nell heard him asking the next family about their arrangements to get to the New Jersey docks.

"New Jersey?" Nell said, loudly enough for her mother to hear above the staccato calls of the men who lined the sides of the walkway.

"That's for people taking trains. We go back to New York, to the docks where we saw your Da," Mama said firmly. "Don't listen to any of them, Nell. Keep an eye on Granny Rose." Nell swallowed hard, realizing it had been a minute or two since she had even glanced at her grandmother. She hooked her arm through Granny Rose's, then glanced back to spot Mary. She and her brothers had fallen back a little. They weren't talking to any of the men either, but Nell saw that others were. Without meeting any of their eyes, Nell watched the men as the line slowed, then stopped.

A gray-haired man came bustling up to Mama. She held up one hand, but he ignored it and came closer anyway. "I just want to warn you to stay away from these men," he said quietly. "You remind me of my wife; she's a decent, kind-hearted woman. You look a lot like her, actually. She was pretty like you are."

"Get away from my mother, sir." Patrick growled from behind them and Nell looked at him. His face was set like stone, his jaw and shoulders squared. "My father will not like to hear that you were bothering her."

The man hesitated, but Mama was glaring at him, too, the expression of hostility on her face clear and unwavering. Nell wanted to apologize to him. He wasn't asking for baggage or anything. He wasn't a thief. Abruptly he cursed, spitting words at Mama that Nell had never heard in her life. Patrick lunged forward but the man skipped backward, disappearing deftly into the crowd.

"How did you know he wasn't telling the truth," Nell asked her mother.

Mama bristled. "I assume them all to be liars just now. Look at them, running out here to act like they are helping us. Decent men have more to do than stand around here all day."

Nell nodded. Granny Rose was beginning to lean on her a little. Nell felt sorry for her. She was exhausted but trying so hard to stand up straight. Little Fiona was sound asleep again.

"Move along, please!" came the shout. The line began to move forward again. Nell kept her eyes down and held tightly to Granny Rose's arm. Mama led the way, her head high, Fiona clutched tightly. Patrick stayed closer now. They were walking almost in formation, their steps timed so closely together that no one could come between them or stop one of them without stopping them all.

The men on both sides of the walkway continued their wheedling and talking in so many languages that it dizzied Nell the way the conversations in the ship's corridor had. The voices seemed to swirl, to ebb and flow like the seawater that was only a few paces behind them. She wasn't finished yet, she reminded herself. Not until she got back to the other side of the bay again to meet her father. That would be the end of the journey: hugging Da.

"What are they looking at?" Patrick murmured.

Nell looked up at him sharply, keeping a tight grip on her grandmother's arm. "Who?"

He gestured with his shin. "Those two, up by the doors."

Nell glanced in the direction he had indicated. There were two men standing side by side, not talking, not moving, Their eyes were fixed on the line of people walking past them. They wore good serge suits, better suits than any of the men who had tried to approach Mama. "Maybe they are just waiting for someone?" Nell said tentatively.

Patrick shook his head. "Watch."

Nell kept watching the two men as the line advanced. "They are waiting for someone," she said finally. "They aren't trying to steal or anything,"

Patrick tilted his head the way he always did when something puzzled him. "No, they aren't thieves, but—"

He stopped so abruptly that Nell turned to look at the men again. One of them had stepped forward. He had something in his hand. He reached out, making a swiping motion at a man who was limping past slowly, trying to steady himself on a young boy who walked beside him. Nell saw a mark appear on the limping man's coat.

"Why would he do that?" Nell wondered aloud.

"Do what?" Granny Rose asked sharply.

"He marked that man's jacket with something."

Granny Rose looked ahead, squinting. "I can't see a mark."

"There is one," Nell said. "And I saw him do it."

"He had better not try to ruin my coat," Granny Rose said slowly.

Patrick and Nell exchanged a look. It was much nicer to have Granny Rose like this—bossy and stern and sure of herself, not lost and confused about things. She was familiar this way. Nell said a silent prayer that it would last, at least until they had passed through all the inspectors and were back with Da on the other side of the gray water.

A swirl of wind came scuttling beneath the roof overhead. Nell shivered, stamping her feet a few times each before the line started moving again.

"This is all nonsense," Granny Rose said as they moved forward again.

Nell didn't answer, but she squeezed her grandmother's arm. If she was tired and cold, Granny Rose must be even worse because of her age. Nell glanced back and was startled when she couldn't see Mary and her brothers at all.

"Nell," Patrick said.

She turned to face front and was startled a second time. The line had moved forward and she and Granny Rose had fallen behind. She nudged her grandmother forward until they had caught up, then she glanced backward again.

"What's wrong, Nell?" Granny Rose asked. They stepped forward once more. They were getting very close to the doors.

"I can't see Mary," Nell explained. "My friend from the ship."

"She'll turn up," Granny Rose said comfortingly.

Nell looked back once more then had to turn around. They were going in. She blinked as they passed through the doorway. The building seemed even bigger inside than it had from the outside.

"Baggage checked there," a man in uniform was saying over and over, pointing, waving people to the left. Mama followed the crowd, but not on the heels of the family in front of them. She held back a little.

"Hurry, Mama," Patrick said from behind them. Nell glanced back. He was carrying his bag and Mama's, but he was walking easily, as though they weighed nothing at all. Nell envied him. Her bag felt like it was full of lead.

"No hurrying," Mama said sternly. "Keep together and stay clear of the crowds. Pickpockets," she said knowingly.

Nell remembered, now that Mama had said it, that her father's last letter had warned them about pickpockets. Mama had had to explain. It was still hard to believe that there were people who could reach down into your pockets and take your money without you knowing it.

"I forgot," Patrick said absently. He was looking up at the ceiling, then back at the rows of windows inside the arches behind them. Above their heads were electric lights. It was odd, how white the light coming from the white glass globes was. Nell kept a tight hold on Granny Rose's arm and tried to watch where she was going. It was hard. She stumbled a little and Granny Rose nearly fell. Mama glanced back.

"Patrick, can you take Nell's bag, too?"

Nell stopped, letting go of Granny Rose's arm long enough to slide the strap off her shoulder. It ached instantly when the pressure of the bag's weight was gone. "Thank you," Nell murmured.

Patrick said something she couldn't quite understand as he picked up her bag and started forward again. It was noisy. People were talking loudly to be heard over each other's voices. Mama followed Patrick. Nell and Granny Rose brought up the rear now.

Ahead of them, Nell saw the limping man and his son standing off to one side. A uniformed man was talking to them brusquely, his face cold and impersonal. Then he turned on his heel and walked off, gesturing for the limping man to follow him. As the man turned to do so, Nell saw the back of his dark coat and the mark upon it. It was an L. An L for limping? Nell flinched. For *lame*? That was cruel.

"That one will be going home tomorrow," someone nearby said. Nell looked up to see a woman standing with three others who looked so much like her they had to be sisters.

"Will they send him back?" Nell asked, half turning to hear the woman's answer as the line moved forward.

"Oh, yes, dear. Anyone who might end up too poorly to fend for himself. They don't want people likely to become wards of the state, you see? Looking for charity."

Nell nodded a vague thanks and guided Granny Rose forward again, then stopped behind Mama and Patrick as the line slowed, then halted. *Anyone who couldn't work?* But that could mean any of the old people. Granny Rose could hardly be expected to work. At home she had helped milk the cows and was the best spinner in the valley. But she did these things at her own pace now. She couldn't work hard anymore.

Uneasy, Nell looked around the room. There were hundreds of people, maybe thousands, and she knew the line still extended out the front door and out to the walkway and beyond. She scanned the faces. There weren't all that many old people, she realized. Some, but not too many. Did they send them all home? How could they do that? Surely Da would have asked. He would have known that his mother wouldn't be let in and he would have told them all to stay at home. But, Nell wondered, what if he hadn't known? What if things had changed since he'd come through this building two years before?

Nell hurried Granny Rose along until they reached the long counter with uniformed men behind it. Mama spoke to the man. Nell couldn't hear what they said, but it was obvious enough. Patrick hoisted the bags up onto the countertop. The man looped stringed tags through the handles like the conductor on the train had on their way to Liverpool. He gave Mama three tags. Nell knew they had numbers on them. The numbers on Mama's tags would match the ones on the bags—that was how the men would know which bags were theirs when they were ready to leave.

"Nell!" Patrick said, and she realized that he had said her name two or three time before she had heard him over the din.

"What?"

"He says you can leave your coat here with the bags if you want to."

Nell shook her head. She was just beginning to thaw; the barely noticeable tingle in her numb feet would turn to an ache soon enough. She didn't want to part with her coat.

"No coats," Mama said loudly to the man. "Is there a place to buy a little food here? A little tea?"

The man only pointed. "Move along, please."

"I would like a cup of tea," Granny Rose piped up. Her voice had a shrill edge that made Nell cringe. She pulled at Granny Rose's arm, trying to get her started in the direction the man had indicated.

"Wait," Mama said suddenly.

Nell looked up and followed her mother's gaze. On the far side of the counter, a man was talking loudly in a language that Nell couldn't understand, but he was looking at the mass of bags and trunks in obvious frustration as the clerk walked back and forth, holding his tag. He looked up and shook his head. The man slapped his own forehead with an open palm, his face flushed dark red with anger.

"We'll take our bags with us after all," Mama told the man in a firm, loud voice that Nell heard clearly.

He cursed beneath his breath, but he reached down and picked the bags up one at a time, tearing off the tags. Patrick took his and Mama's, hanging them off both shoulders to balance the weight. Nell took her own.

"Move it along, now," the man said in a low irritated voice.

Nell took Granny Rose's arm and tried to maneuver her out of line.

"Patrick wouldn't like you pulling me along like this," Granny Rose said. Nell had no doubt as to which Patrick her grandmother meant. Granny Rose was getting angry, which usually got worse before it got better. Nell saw the man behind the counter watching them. She glanced around. There were more men in serge suits near the entrance. They were scanning the crowd. Did they have chalk in their pockets, Nell wondered? "Hush, please, Granny Rose," she said quietly. "We'll get tea before long."

"It doesn't seem," Granny Rose said loudly, "like too much to ask."

"Please move along," the man said, pointing

again. Mama started off and glanced back as Nell and Patrick got Granny Rose moving. It didn't last. Granny Rose didn't want to be hurried. She struggled to free herself, wrenching one arm out of Patrick's gentle grip, the other from Nell.

Patrick leaned down into her face. "Granny Rose, you have to come with us now." He took hold of her arm and Nell tried to help, but Granny Rose managed to jerk her arm free again. She slapped Patrick across the face. Nell heard her mother make a sound of dismay, and a second later a man wearing a serge suit approached them. Nell could only stare as he got closer, smiling genially.

"Excuse me," he said in an even, steady voice. "Is there a problem here?" His English was heavily accented—was he American? An inspector?

Mama stepped between him and Granny Rose. "Frozen feet and empty bellies, sir," she said, sighing. "We are all very tired."

"We are that," Granny Rose put in. The man stepped around Mama to look more closely at her tag. "The *Astoria*? You folks hit quite a storm, I was told," he said as though he was a friendly neighbor, chatting to pass the time.

"We did," Granny Rose said. Nell could tell that the man's presence was confusing her.

"We had to wait on the first dock for hours," Nell said loudly enough to draw the man's attention. "One man froze to death. It upset my grandmother. Granny Rose hates hard things like that, sir."

The man smiled suddenly. "My grandmother's name is Rose." He gestured across the hall. "Go on up the stairs over there. We're crowded today. Move along as quick as you can, please."

Nell watched him walk away. Then she and Patrick got Granny Rose moving, taking reluctant little steps as they made their way through the incoming crowd and headed for the end of another line of people waiting to go up the stairs. Nell looked around for Mary but couldn't spot her. There were just too many people pouring into the big room, a thousand faces to search. She finally gave up.

CHAPTER ELEVEN

The stairs were steep. There was a constant stream of people going up single file, hurried along by their own eagerness to get the ordeal over with and the incessant urgings of the men who stood watching, their faces intent and detached.

At the foot of the stairs, Nell saw another man in a serge suit. He was directing the crowd, pushing them along or holding them back—whatever was needed so that they went up the stairs in single file. The sound of voices was a roar that ebbed and rose at intervals. It was deafening.

Nell's bag was awkward and it seemed heavier than it had on the ship. "Take my hand, Granny Rose," she urged as they got closer to the bottom step.

Granny Rose scowled. "I want a cup of tea and a place to sit and rest a minute."

"We can get tea in a while, I think," Nell began, but her grandmother was already shaking her head.

"I can't understand why it is so difficult. I am an old woman. I need my tea."

"Granny Rose," Nell pleaded. Her grandmother was slowing her pace, in spite of the fact that the people behind them were unwilling to give way. Nell could smell the odor of wet wool and perspiration so strongly from the man behind her that it unsettled her stomach. They probably didn't smell any better, she knew, but she still wanted nothing more than to get away from the unfamiliar smell of an unbathed stranger.

Mama, even with the weight of Fiona to slow her, was getting ahead of them. "Let's keep up," Nell said gently. "We can manage if we try."

"Don't speak to me as though I am a child!" Granny Rose responded sharply.

"Mother Dunne!" Mama exploded. She was wrestling with Fiona, too, glaring. Nell looked at her sister's flushed face. She wasn't crying yet but she would be soon unless Mama could nurse her.

Granny Rose drew herself up and slowed even more, frowning. Nell bit at her lower lip, praying that Granny Rose would calm down.

"We need to climb these stairs," Mama said very slowly and clearly. "Nell needs your help."

Nell blinked, surprised, but then she shot Mama a look of understanding. "Would you give me your hand to steady me?" Nell said politely. Granny Rose eyed her suspiciously, but then she extended her hand and began to walk again. Nell took it just in time, the instant they reached the bottom stair. Granny Rose started upward and stumbled. Patrick caught at the back of her coat and Nell pulled her upright. She didn't say a word, but she regained her balance and started upward again. Nell almost smiled as she matched the rhythm of her stair climbing to Granny Rose's. This was what Granny Rose was famous for to all who had ever known or crossed her: stubborn courage.

"Single file!" the man shouted at them.

Nell blinked. He came closer, pointing and gesturing.

"Do you speak English?" he demanded. Nell nodded. "Then single file, please. One at a time." He said the last few words slowly as though he were speaking to a fool. Nell felt herself blushing.

"The old woman needs a bit of steadying," Mama said politely to the man.

He just shook his head; he looked angry now. "Move along. There are two or three thousand behind you to come through before nightfall." He looked at Nell. "Follow your mother. Then the old woman, then him." He jabbed a finger at Patrick and gestured impatiently at Mama to lead off.

Nell started up the stairs after her. Mama was going as slowly as she could to spare Granny Rose.

There were angry voices behind them, but Nell couldn't understand what was being said, so she couldn't tell if the people were angry with the few seconds of delay, or if something else entirely was going on.

Nell watched Granny Rose struggling with her skirts and timed her own steps to let her grandmother pause on every step, falling behind Mama by one stair. She glanced back. The man in the smelly wool coat came behind Patrick. His hair was plastered down with sweat. Behind him, a person stood on every step, all the way to the bottom. There the crowd widened again, the people standing shoulder to shoulder. Nell kept the pace slow, turning to check Granny Rose every few seconds. When her grandmother placed her foot wrong again, Nell was ready and spun around to keep her upright, a hand on each of her shoulders. Patrick steadied her from behind.

"Stop pushing," Granny Rose said, a deep frown on her face.

"Do look where you are going, Granny Rose," Nell pleaded, afraid her grandmother would fall if she didn't calm down. Granny turned back and Nell shifted her bag higher on her shoulder. It was hard to manage her skirts. Granny Rose and Mama were having the same problem, she could tell. The steep stairs made it all too possible to stumble. Mama had shifted Fiona to her hip, the oversized wrap of Patrick's spare jacket sliding off Fiona's little shoulders, the makeshift stocking leggings sagging and loose. But with one hand free, Mama could at least lift her skirts a little.

"Are you all right?" Mama said, shouting over her shoulder.

"We are," Patrick assured her.

"Yes," Nell added, knowing Mama was afraid to turn and look for herself. "Granny Rose, too."

Granny Rose didn't answer. She was concentrating on the seemingly endless steps now.

Nell felt the muscles in the tops of her thighs starting to ache. She tried to shrug the bag strap high on her shoulder again and nearly dropped it. Recovering, she hesitated and Granny Rose bumped into her, throwing herself off balance. Nell grabbed at her grandmother's coat and held her upright, but it was hard. She swayed, then caught herself.

There was a sudden hard grip on her shoulder and Nell twisted around to see a man in a suit peering at her. She glanced at his right hand. Chalk. He was holding a piece of blue chalk.

"I'm fine," she said, breathing hard from the weight of the bag and her own fear. He hesitated, looking a little surprised that she spoke English.

"I'm fine and strong," Nell said. "I can run like a deer, usually. And my grandmother is the same. Strong and sturdy for her age. We're just very tired."

The man was staring, and Nell pressed her lips together to keep from going on and on—she was starting to sound like a liar, she knew, saying the same thing six ways. It was just the thunder of her heart in her chest. Suddenly the man smiled and nodded. "Go on then, Miss."

Mama had paused and Nell made sure Granny Rose was all right, then, shooting a look at Patrick, she took three quick steps upward to catch up. The man made his way back to his station by the wall. Nell felt her heart pounding. She wasn't sure whether the man had been about to mark her, Granny Rose, or both of them. And she wasn't sure what the marks were, but she knew this much: They were bad. Anyone with a marked coat was not going to be passed through quickly or easily.

"I can barely lift my legs," Granny Rose muttered as she closed the distance and came up behind Nell again. Nell quickened her pace just enough to stay one stair ahead of her.

"Mine hurt, too," Nell said over her shoulder. "Just a little farther."

They turned a corner on a landing, then started upward again. Granny Rose was slowing. Nell looked ahead. There was another man stationed at the top of the stairs. He had one hand in his coat pocket. As she watched he moved forward to make a quick mark on the back of a man's jacket.

The emigrant, startled, tried to look back over his right shoulder to see what mark was there, but of course he couldn't. Nell saw that his mouth was open and he was breathing hard. She glanced from the man, to Granny Rose, then back. Bewildered, the man gasped like a fish out of water as a man in a serge suit tapped his shoulder and led him away.

"Where are they taking him?" Nell asked Patrick nearly shouting.

"Who?" he asked, leaning forward so she could hear him better over the babbling of voices all around them.

"That man," she told him, pointing, glancing up the stairs again. But the man was gone. Granny Rose was slowing down again, and Mama, with little glances over her shoulder, made sure that she didn't get much ahead. The line in front of them had kept going, though, until there was a gap of five or six empty stairs in front of Mama.

"What man?" Patrick asked a second time, louder.

Nell shook her head. It was impossible to talk. She gritted her teeth. The man near the top was watching them closely now. Mama stopped and made a show of switching Fiona from one hip to the other, giving Granny Rose a few seconds' rest. Nell felt her heart quiet a little. Mama's courage was not failing any more than her wit.

"Just a little farther and then we can rest," Nell said close to Granny Rose's ear. She nodded without answering. Nell knew she was out of breath. Everyone was.

The man near the top of the stairs watched them pass, his eyes narrowed. But he didn't step forward and his right hand stayed in his pocket. Nell saw Mama glance back once, then turn to go on, her chin high. Granny Rose topped the stairs and Nell stepped up behind her and paused without meaning to. She was standing at the edge of the most astounding room she had ever seen in her life. It was full of people, standing nearly shoulder to shoulder, filling the enormous space. The ceiling was far overhead, high enough to echo the cascade of languages.

"They look like penned sheep," Granny Rose said and Nell could only nod.

CHAPTER TWELVE

"Move along," someone was shouting. The cacophony of voices was almost unbearable. Nell could not stop staring; this room *was* as big as a pasture. Bigger. She stood still, looking straight up as Patrick stepped around her to ask Mama something. Above their heads the ceiling arched upward like a noon sky. There were balconies running around it, and she could see a door here and there along the walkways. Above it were windows shaped in pointed arches, like a church. At the far end a window, shaped like a rising moon, let in the cold gray light of the day outside.

Nell looked up to see a uniformed man with a thick black beard. He came closer, shouting something at Mama. She answered and he pointed. Mama turned to catch Nell's eye, then Patrick's, then she started off. Nell and Patrick fell in on either side of Granny Rose and followed their mother toward the mass of humanity in front of them.

Nell kept glancing upward, until the glint of metal railings in front of them caught her attention and she lowered her eyes. Now she fully understood what Granny Rose had meant. She blinked. There was a maze of iron railings, separating the people into lines that crossed the huge room.

"Nell? NELL! Over here, Nell!"

The shrill sound of Mary's voice pierced the roar of lower voices. Nell searched the crowds ahead of them with her eyes. There. Ten or fifteen people from the end of a long line, Mary stood with her brothers. She put both arms into the air and turned in a circle, a silly dance of joy. Nell grinned back at her, forgetting for a few seconds the weight of her bag and all her fears. Then Mary's brother Will reached out to turn her around. Nell saw a uniformed man in front of them. Nell could just see, finding a line of sight through the crowd, that he was talking to Mary. It was impossible to tell what he was saying, of course, but Nell stared at him anyway, even as she kept walking beside Granny Rose, following her mother across the polished floor.

"IRELAND?" a man shouted, so close to Nell that she jumped. He had hold of her tag and was reading it. As he stepped back, Mama turned and nodded at him. The man reached out and nudged her, pointing, saying something Nell couldn't hear. Mama nodded again and Nell followed once more, making sure that Granny Rose stayed close. Mama came to the end of a line and stopped just short of the pair of iron rails that formed a narrow pathway.

"Hand me my bag," she shouted at Patrick. He slid his bag and Mama's to the floor, then stretched, flexing his shoulders. Nell let her bag drop to the floor. Her shoulder ached. She turned, trying to see Mary again, but couldn't. From here, there were hundreds of people in the way.

"Nell!" Mama shouted. "Help me!"

Nell blinked, turning to look. Mama had laid Fiona down on the floor, using Patrick's jacket as a blanket. Mama was holding Fiona still with one hand on her chest as she fished through her bag. Nell understood what she was looking for and took over.

The cloths they had brought for Fiona's diapers were all stale smelling, but at least they were dry. Mama took the one Nell handed her and turned back to Fiona. Her hands flying, Mama undid the pins that held the wet diaper in place and skinned if off. She wrapped it in two more of the dry ones to keep everything in the bag from soaking up the wet, and then buckled her bag closed again. Nell bent to pick up her sister as Mama worked to close her bag.

They were back on their feet and moving forward before anyone had a chance to get angry. Once more, Nell marveled at her mother. Instead of resting, she had been thinking ahead. This had probably been their last chance to change Fiona for hours.

"Where are you coming from?" A man appeared to their right. The line went past him, Nell realized, but he had been invisible to her a moment before. Mama started to show him the papers they had been given by the ship's officers, but he waved them aside. He was staring closely at them, one at a time. His eyes rested longest on Granny Rose. She was still quiet, her eyes down, though her breathing had slowed. Nell felt her skin prickle with sweat as the man looked them over.

"Any pains, Granny?" the man asked.

Granny Rose looked up. "What did you ask me?"

The man nodded pleasantly. "Anyone feel sick? Anyone get sick on the crossing?"

"No," Mama said flatly, before anyone else could speak.

The inspector smiled again. "I just wondered if Granny here has any pains and aches. Do you?"

Nell stared at him, a little confused. He was speaking in a lowered voice and she could barely hear him. But Granny Rose looked up. "No, young man. You're asking rude questions."

Nell waited for the inspector to get irritated, but he didn't. He smiled wider. "If you can hear me, raise your right hand," he said it so quietly that Nell wasn't sure she had understood, but she raised her hand when Patrick and her mother did. Granny Rose scowled, but raised hers, too. The inspector asked for their identification cards. Mama handed Fiona to Nell, then got the cards from her pocket and gave them to him. He glanced at them and handed them back. "Move along, please."

They picked up their bags and walked on. Nell glanced back. There were people coming into the railed aisle right behind them and the line stretched back from there. She could just see the top of the stairs through the crowd. People were marching up in pairs now, not single file. Perhaps the line below had gotten too backed up and they were trying to hurry people upstairs?

Granny Rose was right, it was like sheep pens. It also reminded Nell of the big train stations she had seen getting to Liverpool. But this was different, she knew. There was no guarantee that they would be allowed to go where they wanted to go.

"Will you open your collars, please?" Nell heard someone say. Another inspector was facing them, his voice a monotone of polite inquiry. Nell set her bag down and moved to one side to allow Patrick room enough to put down the two bags he carried. Mama unbuttoned her coat, but the man was motioning at her. "The dress collar, too, please."

Nell's stomach tightened. Were they going to be examined like this, *here*, with a thousand people all around them?

The inspector leaned forward, looking at their throats. He reached out and touched Granny Rose's cheek, gently turning her head. Then he gestured, "Move on, please."

"What could be wrong with our throats?" Patrick muttered as they picked up the bags. Nell shook her head, her heart pounding. She had seen Granny Rose's fists clench when the man had touched her. And she was walking like she always did when she was angry, stiff kneed and rigidly erect.

Nell edged forward as the line moved, looking back at the group of people behind them. They had all opened the collars. The last woman was unwinding a long scarf and Nell caught her breath. The woman's throat was terribly swollen, bulging outward drastically.

"Goiter," Mama said, turning back and noticing Nell's horrified expression.

"What causes it?" Nell asked, looking away from the woman, who was weeping now.

Mama shrugged impatiently. "I don't know, Nell. The doctors don't know either." Fiona was fussing now. Mama was jiggling her up and down, trying to soothe her, but Nell knew it wasn't going to work for long. Fiona was hungry and sick of being held still. At home she would have spent her day toddling about the house, happily following them as they did their chores. Nell looked closely at her little sister.

She looked pale now, and her eyes were reddish from fussing.

"This is nonsense," Granny Rose said loudly, turning to face Nell.

"It is," Nell agreed, trying to smile agreeably. "But once we are finished we can go meet Da."

"And Patrick," Granny Rose said insistently. "Your grandfather will be pleased to see what a pretty girl you have become." She shook her head. "I have missed that old man, you know. And Sean."

Nell nodded, understanding something for the first time. Grandpa had died only about six months before her father had left for America. Maybe it was easier for Granny Rose to imagine that Grandpa had gone with him—that he was in America, not heaven, and that she would soon see him again. Nell pulled in a long, deep breath, wishing once more that she were home, that they all were.

"Open your blouses, please," came a loud voice. Nell leaned to see around her brother. The people in front of them were fumbling with buttons. The women were blushing and their eyes were down. The inspector had a doctor's instrument around his neck. It had earpieces and he put them in his ears, then leaned forward to place the other end on each person's chest. He tipped his head as if listening and Nell wondered how he could hear anything over the roar of voices. "Move along, please," he said, straightening.

Nell gritted her teeth as they moved forward and the inspector repeated his request. Granny Rose had been shuffling along without looking up, but now she raised her head and Nell could see her bristling with anger.

"Open your blouses," the man repeated. He added a pantomime in case they spoke no English.

"Please now, Granny Rose," Mama said quietly. "Everyone has to do this. They want to make sure we are healthy."

"Of course we are healthy," Granny Rose snapped at the inspector as though he had said it, not Mama.

"I have to check, ma'am," he said politely.

"You will do no such thing. Not to me or to my granddaughter." She nodded toward Mama. "That one can do as she pleases, she's old enough."

Nell set her bag down. Patrick was unbuttoning his shirt again, but he was glancing nervously over the heads of the crowd, clearly embarrassed, and bothered that his mother and sister were about to do the same in public.

"It will take no more than a moment," the inspector said. His voice was polite, but Nell could see that he was not as patient as he sounded. His jaw was clenched so tightly she could see a muscle working in the side of his face.

"Everyone has to do it," she said, leaning close to her grandmother's ear.

Granny Rose was incredulous. "Patrick is not going to like this. He won't stand for—"

"We won't tell him," Nell said impulsively. She was trying to fumble her dress buttons open while she talked to Granny Rose. She glanced up just as the inspector finished with Fiona. Patrick gestured and the man placed the instrument on his chest.

Biting at her lip, ignoring Granny Rose's hand on her arm, Nell stepped forward and felt the cold steel of the round instrument on her skin. Blushing furiously, she stood still while the doctor listened to her heart, then straightened again. She glanced up to see a boy her own age staring at her. She glared at him and he looked away. Her hands shook, rebuttoning. Then she took Fiona from her mother. Mama stepped forward, too, standing stolidly until the doctor was through. And then it was Granny Rose's turn.

"Let me help you," Nell said. She passed Fiona to Patrick once his shirt was closed. Then she reached for the buttons that ran down the front of her grandmother's dress. Granny Rose swatted her hands away.

"We don't have all day," the inspector said tersely.

Mama came forward. "She is old and very modest and—"

"I can see that," the man said, cutting Mama off.

"Granny Rose, please," Nell begged. "It only takes a second and people are waiting."

"Where's Patrick?" Granny Rose demanded. Her eyes were desperate now. "Patrick?" she called the name at the top of her voice. The cry was lost in the noise of the crowd. She rounded on Mama. "Where is he?"

Without warning, the inspector leaned forward and grabbed Granny Rose's hand. He trapped her wrist, pressing his thumb against the blue veins that showed through her skin. Then he lifted her arm, turning her like a puppet. His right hand darted into his pocket and pulled out chalk. Before anyone could say another word, he had slashed a blue-chalk X high on Granny Rose's right shoulder.

Nell looked at her mother and saw the anguish in her eyes. Nell blinked back tears. She should have been more patient, should have thought up something clever to tell Granny Rose—she should have done *something*. Now Granny Rose was going to be sent home, and Nell knew she would have to go with her. The idea of having to leave while the rest of her family stayed in America made her heart ache. In a flashing instant it was clear to her that something had changed inside her heart. She loved Ireland and she always would. But she wanted to live in this shiny new place with the huge buildings and the fairy snow, too.

"Move along," the inspector growled. Granny Rose stared at him, furious, her head high and her eyes fierce.

"You have Patrick locked up somewhere, don't you?" she accused, slapping the iron rail.

The inspector took a step backward and glanced at Mama. "Move her along, please, Madam."

Mama reached out and took Granny Rose's arm. "Don't be foolish," she scolded gently. "Patrick is waiting for us, just up ahead here. Once we are finished, we can . . . " Her voice trailed off as she managed to turn Granny Rose and get her walking. The railed aisle was empty for fully fifteen or twenty feet ahead of them—they had fallen far behind the people in front of them.

Nell stood a second, tears building up in her eyes. This was her fault. She had not done the job that Da had asked her to do. She was so tired and the noise of the voices hammered at her ears. How had she let this happen?

CHAPTER THIRTEEN

Nell walked numbly, holding Fiona when an inspector asked Mama to step close, then handing her back. She bent her head while one man rifled through her hair, searching for something she could only hope wasn't there. If it was, he didn't say a word, just motioned them on when he finished with Granny Rose. She had gone quiet again. Nell clenched her teeth as she picked up her bag and went a few feet, then set it down again.

A scream ahead of them jolted her out of her daze. She leaned to one side to see around Mama and caught her breath. An inspector was bent over a little boy, jabbing at his eyes with something that looked like a buttonhook. The boy wriggled and screamed while his mother held his hand and pleaded with him in a language Nell didn't recognize.

The next three people in the party stood bravely, and Nell could see what the man was doing. Using the buttonhook, he was deftly turning up people's eyelids and peering at the pink underside. It was done in an instant. Nell held her breath, terrified, both for herself and because Granny Rose was likely to put up a fight again.

When their turn came, Patrick went first, then Mama. They both managed not to cry out, pressing their lips together hard. Fiona cried hard, but quieted fairly quickly. Nell kept a tight hold on Granny Rose's arm, talking in her ear as they stood side by side.

"See that? Only the babies cry. I suppose they have to check our eyes for some disease. It can't hurt as much as it looks like it would," she added as they got close. "Do you want me to go first, Granny Rose?"

Her grandmother stood stolidly in the line and answered without looking at her. "No. They don't scare me."

Nell nodded slowly, saying a silent prayer. From what she had said, it was impossible to tell if Granny Rose was still confused or if she was just being her stubborn and brave self.

Nell watched, ready to take her grandmother's hand, while the inspector examined her eyes. Granny Rose did not flinch or cry out at all. Afterward, she squeezed her eyes shut, and then opened them without speaking. Mama pulled Granny Rose gently forward and it was Nell's turn.

It was horribly painful, but the pain lasted for an

instant, no more, in each eye. The inspector was lightning fast. He stepped back and motioned Nell to move on, already lifting the hook as he turned.

After the buttonhook, nothing else seemed too terrible. Even Granny Rose seemed calm as they walked slowly through the maze of aisles, going wherever they were pushed, following an endless chain of pointing fingers and impatient instructions. But it wasn't going to matter, Nell knew, walking behind her grandmother, thinking about the blue chalk mark that had changed everything. Passing all the rest of the medical inspections wouldn't matter for her or for Granny Rose. Not now.

The noise was dizzying and Nell found herself regarding the roar as though it was somehow a deep silence that few sounds and few voices could penetrate. She kept her eyes on the inspectors, Granny Rose, strangers' faces—anything but Mama's face. Since the inspector had put the mark on Granny Rose's shoulder, all the starch had left Mama's posture. She shuffled along like a sleepwalker except that her eyes were desperate.

With Fiona whimpering in her arms, Mama led the way past the last medical inspector and turned, following the people in front of them, toward a line of tall desks at the back of the room. As they walked forward, Nell realized that the iron rails that had held her prisoner for what felt like a lifetime were now gone. She was able to walk beside her grandmother again. Patrick stayed close, too, as they approached the bored-looking man at the high desk.

"Coming from Ireland?" he said, taking the papers Mama handed him. She nodded. Nell glanced at Granny Rose. She was standing still, but her lips were moving. She was talking to herself. It was something she had always done, but now Nell realized how odd it looked. She stepped forward to stand so that the man behind the desk couldn't see Granny Rose.

The inspector was looking at their papers, running his finger down a list on his desk. He looked up. "Are you and your family all Catholic?"

Mama nodded.

Nell stood quietly, her heart pounding, as the man began to fire off questions that Mama answered slowly and carefully. He wanted to know what kind of work they each knew how to do. He wondered about Mama's political beliefs, then about Da and how long he had been in America. He asked if she had ever been divorced, how many children she still had in Ireland, if any.

Nell's heart lightened a little as the man spoke. He seemed to be reading a standard list of questions. Looking down the line at other desks, Nell saw people embracing, waving stamped inspection cards over their heads. This was it, then, the end of the line. And no one had approached them about the mark. Maybe the mark on Granny Rose's shoulder meant something different—just that she was argumentative or something.

"Passports?" the man was saying.

Mama dug into her coat pockets once more. Nell knew that their passports were in good order. There was nothing to fear there.

"Excuse me?"

The brusque voice startled Nell into turning around. A man in a uniform was behind Granny Rose, reaching to touch her shoulder. Nell stiffened.

"Come this way, please," he was saying, not to all of them this time, but to Granny Rose.

"She is with us," Nell said haltingly. The man nodded, but didn't look up.

"You can wait here for her. It won't take long," he said evenly.

Granny Rose turned to look at him and her eyes were narrowed. "May I go with her, please?" Nell said quietly. "She will feel safer if one of us can come along."

"Please, sir," Mama put in. "My daughter is finished with all the inspections and there is no further examination here for her, is there?" She looked pleadingly up at the man behind the desk.

He shook his head. "There's nothing that her mother can't answer for her." He made a sweeping motion with one hand, as though Nell was something he could brush away at will. Nell slid her bag off her shoulder and left it next to Patrick. He smiled encouragingly and she loved him for it. But then her eyes began to sting so she looked away.

"Follow me," the man was saying. He strode off and Nell reached for Granny Rose's arm.

"What is he doing with us?" Granny Rose demanded as they started off. Nell tried to think clearly. If she told Granny Rose what she feared, it would do no good and might do harm. "They want to ask you a few questions, probably about Da's work and how he was raised," she said finally.

Granny Rose nodded. "That makes sense. If you want to know about a man, ask his mother."

The inspector had stopped and was pointing up a staircase. Nell took a deep breath and looked at her grandmother. "Can you make it up more steps?"

Granny Rose smiled bitterly, looking up the stairway. "And why not? No food or tea since before sunrise. Shall we run up?"

The man didn't act like he had heard her wry joke. He motioned impatiently. Nell tightened her grip on Granny Rose's arm and they started upward. Halfway up Granny Rose was breathing hard, but she didn't stop or slow. It struck Nell how odd it was, to be able to hear Granny Rose's breath, their footsteps. Then she realized that the noise of the room below was receding with every step they took.

At the top of the stairs, the man gestured at an open door. Scared, Nell ushered her grandmother inside. The room was strange and silent as the inspector closed the door behind them.

This one man was tall and thin, with sandy hair and brown eyes that reminded Nell of home. His uniform was the same as all the others. He seated Granny Rose and asked for Nell to wait by the door. Nell watched helplessly as he directed Granny Rose to draw a diamond shape, then to put wooden blocks in a square. Granny Rose was patient at first, but her irritation began to show when he handed her a puzzle.

"If you are going to ask me about Sean, let's get to it," she said angrily, setting the puzzle down on the table.

The man asked her politely to do the puzzle, but she refused, shaking her head. "Sean is a very good boy. His father is a fine man, too."

"Who is Sean?" the inspector asked.

Nell felt her eyes sting. She had told Granny Rose exactly the wrong thing. Now she would be upset and start raving at the inspector. She would convince him she was not able to think clearly anymore. And they would send her home.

"Who is Sean?" the inspector repeated.

Granny Rose glared at him, tilting her head. "Are you pretending you don't know?"

"Sean is my father," Nell said, walking closer.

"My father is Granny Rose's son. He's been in New York two years and has a fine job."

"A fine job and his employer values him highly," Granny Rose added, still frowning at the man.

"Are the two of you traveling alone?" the man asked.

"No," Nell said before Granny Rose could snap at him again. "There's my mother and my baby sister and my older brother, too."

"How old is the older brother?"

Nell took in a breath, glad he was focusing on her now, but terrified she would say the wrong thing. "He's fifteen, nearly sixteen," Nell said. "Tall for his age and strong," she added.

The man nodded. "You know why your grandmother was sent up here?"

Nell nodded cautiously, glancing at Granny Rose. "At home she milked cows and made cheese," Nell said quietly, looking into his eyes and willing him to understand. "She takes care of my sister, Fiona, while Mama does chores as well. She bakes the bread and tends the fire. This is all just—" she spread her hands wide, trying to find words that would explain. "This is all very different from home."

"Your mother trusts her with a baby?"

Nell nodded. "Oh, yes, sir, and Granny Rose is admired by everyone in—"

"Hush, child!" Granny Rose interrupted. "He

wanted to hear about Sean."

"I told her that on the way up here," Nell whispered, blushing at her fib, but not wanting the man to think Granny Rose was making things up.

"If someone did have to take a return journey, you'd be the one to go, too?" the man asked quietly.

Nell nodded miserably. So he was going to send Granny Rose home, he just needed to know who was going to go with her. "My father has always cared for his family," Nell said quietly, remembering what the woman had said downstairs. "He sent us money to come and my brother Patrick is nearly a man now."

"Patrick is the finest man God ever made," Granny Rose broke in. "There's never been another like him. Where is he?"

Without answering her, the inspector handed the puzzle back to Granny Rose and asked her politely to put it together. This time she did, quickly and deftly and angrily, as though the test were an insult. The inspector motioned Nell to one side.

"We will all take care of Granny Rose," Nell said earnestly in a whisper before she could speak. "No one in my family has ever been on charity. My da would die first. There's not a lazy one among us either." She pulled in a breath, her heart slamming at her ribs. "Nor a dishonest one," she whispered. "No one ever in jail. My da is a good man."

"My Sean is that," Granny Rose added.

The inspector laughed. "And nothing wrong with her hearing."

"Nor any other part of me," Granny Rose said.

"We will take care of her as she gets older, too," Nell whispered, barely breathing the words now.

The inspector looked into her eyes. "I believe you. I think the Dunnes will be good American citizens."

He walked back to his desk and pulled out a card. He filled it out quickly, his pen scratching over the paper. Then he stamped it and pinned it to Granny Rose's coat above the blue-chalk mark. She twisted around.

"What's that?"

He glanced at Nell. "Your granddaughter will explain it, Ma'am. She's a smart one."

"That she is," Granny Rose agreed, getting up. She started the wrong way for the door, but Nell hurried to steer her along. She glanced back and the inspector nodded absently and looked down at a list on his desk. Then he followed them to the door. There were three people waiting on the landing. Nell followed Granny Rose past them and they headed down the stairs. At the bottom, Granny Rose turned the wrong way again and Nell guided back in the right direction. As they turned the corner, Nell saw Mama and Patrick standing near the wall, waiting. Their heads were down and they weren't talking at all.

The noise made it impossible to call to them, but Mama looked up and Nell danced a little circle, her joy almost more than she could stand. Mama began to smile and she nudged Patrick. Nell turned a dance for him, too, drawing stares from strangers and a frown from Granny Rose. It didn't matter, nothing mattered. In an hour or two, she would see her father. They would go to their new home somewhere in the fairy city of New York, America, together, a proper family again. Even the noise of the room seemed less over-whelming, muted by the singing in her heart.

February 14, 1904
Home on Madison Street

I did not write yesterday because there was too much to do. But today I can record all the wonderful things that have happened. The house Papa found is small but well built and pretty. There are roses in the front yard for Mama to tend and enough room for a little garden come summer. Da is so proud and so happy to have us here. We are all still wandering in a dream. We took a ride on one of the tunnel trains this morning. It is like a miracle. You climb on and poof! Before you can think, you have gone a mile.

We went to a place where employers come to hire men—Battery Park. Patrick talked to a few and will go back tomorrow to talk to more. But the best part of going was that I saw Angus! He has given me their address and says he will give Mary mine. So we will be friends forever. Oh, I do hope so.

Our house is pleasant and clean and we have electric lights! Two little ones in the parlor and one in the kitchen. They are the clearest, purest white! Granny Rose is baffled by them, but she will learn. She was confused again this morning, but Da talked her into laughing a bit and she forgot about finding Granddad.

Da is so glad she wasn't sent home. This way we can take good care of her, he says. We will all try our best, that much I know. The inspector was right. The Dunnes are going to make very good Americans.

Sometimes one day can change a life forever

American Diaries

Different girls,
living in different periods of America's past,
reveal their hearts' secrets in the pages
of their diaries. Each one faces a challenge
that will change her life forever.
Don't miss any of their stories:

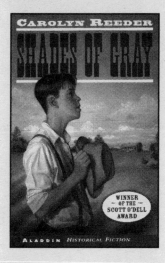

The past comes ALIVE

in stirring historical fiction from ALADDIN PAPERBACKS

Brothers of the Heart
Joan W. Blos
0-689-71724-5
$4.99 US
$6.99 Canadian

Caddie Woodlawn
Carol Ryrie Brink
0-689-71370-3
$4.99 US
$6.99 Canadian

Forty Acres and Maybe a Mule
Harriette Gillem Robinet
0-689-83317-2
$4.99 US
$6.99 Canadian

A Gathering of Days
Joan W. Blos
0-689-82991-4
$4.99 US
$6.99 Canadian

Hope
Louann Gaeddert
0-689-80382-6
$3.99 US
$4.99 Canadian

Shades of Gray
Carolyn Reeder
0-689-82696-6
$4.99 US
$6.99 Canadian

Steal Away Home
Lois Ruby
0-689-82435-1
$4.50 US
$6.50 Canadian

The Second Mrs. Giaconda
E. L. Konigsburg
0-689-82121-2
$4.50 US
$5.99 Canadian

The Best Bad Thing
Yoshiko Uchida
0-689-71745-8
$4.99 US
$6.99 Canadian

A Jar of Dreams
Yoshiko Uchida
0-689-71672-9
$4.95 US
$6.95 Canadian

The Journey Home
Yoshiko Uchida
0-689-71641-9
$4.99 US
$6.99 Canadian

The Eternal Spring of Mr Ito
Sheila Garrigue
0-689-71809-8
$4.99 US
$6.99 Canadian

Under the Shadow of Wings
Sara Harrell Banks
0-689-82436-X
$4.99 US
$6.99 Canadian

The Journey to America Saga
Sonia Levitin
Annie's Promise
0-689-80440-7
Journey to America
0-689-71130-1
Silver Days
0-689-71570-6
All $4.99 US
$6.99 Canadian

Aladdin Paperbacks • Simon & Schuster Children's Publishing • www.SimonSaysKids.com